PUFFIN BOOKS

STARSHIP *TRAVELLER*

Sucked through the appalling nightmare of the Seltsian Void, the starship *Traveller* emerges at the other side of the black hole into an unknown universe. YOU are the captain of the *Traveller* and her fate lies in your hands. Will you be able to discover the way back to Earth from the alien peoples and planets you encounter, or will you and your crew be doomed to roam uncharted space forever?

Steve Jackson, co-founder of the highly successful Games Workshop, has created a thrilling adventure amongst the stars. There are three new forms of combat to be used, a full ship's crew and an adventure sheet to record your gains and losses. All *you* need is two dice, a pencil and an eraser.

Four more Fighting Fantasy Gamebooks are published in Puffin: *The Warlock of Firetop Mountain*, *The Citadel of Chaos*, *The Forest of Doom* and *City of Thieves*.

D0843648

Steve Jackson

STARSHIP TRAVELLER

Illustrated by Peter Andrew Jones

Puffin Books

Puffin Books, Penguin Books Ltd, Harmondsworth, Middlesex, England
Penguin Books, 40 West 23rd Street, New York, New York 10010, U.S.A.
Penguin Books Australia Ltd, Ringwood, Victoria, Australia
Penguin Books Canada Ltd, 2801 John Street, Markham, Ontario, Canada L3R 1B4
Penguin Books (N.Z.) Ltd, 182–190 Wairau Road, Auckland 10, New Zealand

First published 1983
Reprinted 1983 (seven times)
Reprinted 1984 (twice)

Printed and bound in Great Britain by
Cox & Wyman Ltd, Reading
Set in Linotron Palatino by
Rowland Phototypesetting Ltd,
Bury St Edmunds, Suffolk

To

Tony A, Terry A, Bryan A, Pete A, Clive B, Ian B, Pete B, Phil B, Gary C, Mary C, Brian C, Peter D-E, Meryl D, Stuart D, Kenneth E, Albie F, Anthony E, Vivienne G, Peter G, Trevor H, Simon H, Claire H, Tony H, Gary H, David H, Karl H, Neil J, Bill J, Jervis J, Lenny J, Shekou K, Gerrard K, Chrissie L, Diane L, Lindsey P, Liz L, Steve L, Dawn L, Malcolm L, Jackie M, Bob M, John M, Abenaa M, Alan M, Jackie M, Laurence M, Rick N, Johnno, Timmo, Rick O, Andy P, Alan P, Michael P, Heather P, Rick P, Colin R, Peter R, Sushma S, Peggy S, Andy S, Keith T, Kathy T, Karl T, Clive T, Jamie T, Ian T, Dom T, Ian W, Gaynor W, Ted W, Tim W, and David W

. . . may they all live long and prosper

CONTENTS

PREPARE FOR
YOUR MISSION

You are Captain of the Starship *Traveller*. The ship itself is the pride of your AstroNavy. Its weapons and defence systems are the most technically advanced in the fleet and its crew are first-rate.

Before you begin your voyage, you must determine the strengths and weaknesses of yourself as Captain and your crew members. The journey through the black hole will do some damage to the weapons and defence systems on the ship.

To determine your starting characteristics, you will need two dice and a pencil to record scores on the *Adventure Sheet* on page 16. Before writing on the *Adventure Sheet*, you may wish to take photocopies for use in future adventures. It is unlikely that you will find the way back to Earth in your first adventure.

Unlike previous Fantasy Gamebooks, you will not find rules for fighting alien creatures and ships here at the beginning of the book. Rules for ship-to-ship, hand-to-hand and phaser (laser pistol) combat are given in the text of the book, to allow you to start playing with minimal delay. As you come across combat situations, you will be referred to sections describing the appropriate combat rules. All you need to do here is roll dice to determine the initial scores on your *Adventure Sheet*.

Your Ship

Roll one die. Add 6 to the roll. Enter this total in the WEAPONS STRENGTH section of your *Adventure Sheet*. When shooting at enemy ships, you will need to roll *lower* than this score to make a hit.

Roll one die. Add 12 to this roll. Enter this total in the SHIELDS section of your *Adventure Sheet*. When enemy ships hit you, you will lose points from this SHIELDS score. Your shields will weaken significantly after a few hits have been taken. If your ship is ever hit when your SHIELDS score is zero, your ship will be destroyed instantly.

You and Your Crew

Personnel will perform according to their SKILL and STAMINA scores. Their SKILL score reflects their abilities within their own profession, i.e. your Science Officer's skill with computers, your Medical Officer's skill as a doctor, your Security Officer's combat ability and your own leadership and decision-making skills as Captain.

On your *Adventure Sheet* you will see entries for your key staff (Captain, Science Officer, Medical Officer, Security Officer and Engineering Officer, together with two security Guards). Repeat the following procedure for each in turn:

Roll one die. Add 6 to the result. Enter the total as that person's SKILL score.

Roll two dice. Add 12 to the result. Enter the total as that person's STAMINA score.

You may now see how each crew member is likely to perform at his/her job; the higher the SKILL score, the better.

Combat

Only security staff are skilled in combat. They will be your obvious choice in hand-to-hand or phaser fighting. Non-security staff may fight, but their skills lie in other areas. If, by choice or through necessity, you wish a non-security crew member to fight an alien, you must deduct 3 points from his or her SKILL score during the battle. This rule applies to your Science Officer, Medical Officer and Engineering Officer only. It does not apply to you, as the ship's Captain. Your own fighting skills are equal to your professional skills, as befits a true hero.

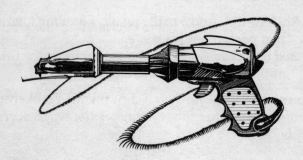

Luck

Every true hero is at the mercy of the forces of chance. You will find a LUCK box on your *Adventure Sheet*. Roll one die, add 6 to the roll and enter the total in this LUCK box.

Call it acts of God, The Force or whatever you will – LUCK will play an important part in your adventure.

Beaming Down on to Planets

When you arrive at a planet, you will be given the option of 'beaming down' on to the surface. Sometimes only you will beam down, but often you will be instructed to choose two or three crew members to accompany you. When given this choice, you may choose only crew members listed on your *Adventure Sheet* (there are some other restrictions limiting your choice – see the 'Losing an Officer' section below). Your Science Officer is a problem-solver, your Medical Officer is a doctor, your Engineering Officer has a knowledge of mechanics and geology and your Security Officer and Guards are your fighters.

Record your choices *before* you land on the planet and remember that only those staff actually in the landing party will be able to act for you while on the surface.

Restoring Stamina

On some planets you may become involved in fights and other situations which drain your STAMINA scores. There are two ways of restoring STAMINA. You may find a planet with superior medical technology able to restore STAMINA. Instructions will be given in the text. You may also restore 2 STAMINA points to each crew member listed on your *Adventure Sheet* every time you leave a planet. However, you may only gain the advantage of this medical treatment if you have your original Medical Officer. If your Medical Officer dies, you may not restore STAMINA in this way. Crew members' STAMINA scores may never exceed their initial value.

Losing an Officer or Security Guard

If, during your adventure, one of the Officers or Guards listed on your *Adventure Sheet* dies or is lost, you must cross him off your *Adventure Sheet* and he may play no further part in the adventure. His position is taken over by his assistant. You must determine the SKILL and STAMINA scores of this newly promoted assistant and then record them on the *Adventure Sheet*. The assistant's SKILL score is equal to the SKILL score of the lost Officer minus 2 points, as this assistant is not as skilful as the Officer he replaces. The assistant's STAMINA score is determined in the normal way, i.e. roll two dice and add 12 to the result.

This newly promoted replacement *may not* be beamed down on to planets or used in any missions where you are instructed to choose a crew member. Being the last available candidate for his particular position, you cannot risk losing him. However, you may use him for routine duties (i.e. where no option is given in the text). A replacement Medical Officer may restore STAMINA to injured crew members on leaving planets (see 'Restoring Stamina' above), but at the reduced rate of 1 STAMINA point per planet.

ADVENTURE SHEET

CREW

CAPTAIN	
SKILL 12	STAMINA 24
SCIENCE OFFICER	
SKILL* 8	STAMINA 18
MEDICAL OFFICER	
SKILL* 8	STAMINA 17
ENGINEERING OFFICER	
SKILL* 9	STAMINA 16
SECURITY OFFICER	
SKILL 9	STAMINA 24

SECURITY GUARD 1		SECURITY GUARD 2	
SKILL 10	STAMINA 22 12	SKILL 10	STAMINA 23

*Deduct 3 points from SKILL in combat

SHIP

WEAPONS STRENGTH	SHIELDS
12	18

NOTES

LUCK
11

Your Adventure Is About To Begin!

The scores you have recorded on your *Adventure Sheet* will give you an indication of the strengths and weaknesses of yourself, your crew and your ship. You need know nothing of how these scores will come into play – all will be explained as necessary as your adventure unfolds.

In the adventure which follows, you are the Captain of the *Traveller*, lost in an unknown universe. Your own skill as a Captain will determine whether you and your crew will ever see Earth again. You are about to be flung through a black hole into unknown space. Your only chance of return will be to find another suitable black hole and guide the ship through it back to your own universe.

You are now ready to set off. Take your seat on the bridge and prepare yourself for the adventure ahead.

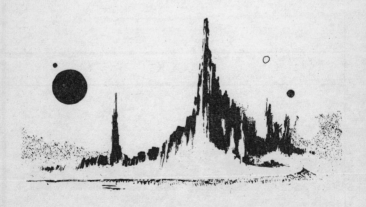

NOW TURN OVER

Panic!

From your seat at the helm of the Starship *Traveller* you study the VDU anxiously. Engineering Section has reported an overdrive malfunction which has locked the warp engines at a 10 per cent velocity gain. You are watching the velocity indicator advancing rapidly through the safe region towards overload. You hit the communicator button and call Engineering for further news . . .

It is not good. The malfunction cannot be traced and it will take another thirteen minutes for a system check to provide a full analysis.

You are heading towards the Seltsian Void, a known black hole. You may or may not avoid it, but your Science Officer has another plan. If you swing the ship through its immense gravitational pull, its gravity drag may help reduce your speed as you travel away from it. This is worth a try, but the navigational tuning will have to be precise . . .

You swing the starship hard to starboard as you enter the Seltsian's gravitational field and fasten your eyes on the velocity indicator. To your great relief the plan seems to be working! The gain comes down from 10 per cent to 5 per cent to zero, to −5 per cent!

Loud cheers come from the crew, but you are still watching the velocity indicator. It is now showing −15 per cent, then −25 per cent and still falling. The ship is being sucked into the Seltsian Void!

You hit the red alert button and instruct all ship's personnel to strap themselves down. The ship begins to whine and shake as it rapidly accelerates towards the black hole. There is nothing you can do to avert the impending disaster.

An almighty explosion rocks the ship and all the crew, including you, lose consciousness. Turn to **256**.

2

You approach the blue planet and take up orbit position. Scanners indicate that the planet is inhabited and that there is considerable development of the planet surface by some intelligent life-form, suggesting a well-organized social structure.

You try various radio frequencies and, after some time, an alien face appears on the screen. Dressed in a uniform of some kind, this creature is humanoid, but thin, with a large, bulbous head and bony fingers. He announces himself as First Officer I-Abail of the National Government of Jolsen 3. You explain your plight and reassure him that you mean no harm. He invites you – but only you – to beam down to his offices.

Will you beam down and visit this planet (turn to **222**) or thank him for his offer, but press onwards (turn to **41**)?

3

The beast roars loudly as the blast strikes at point-blank range. With a violent crash, it topples over, dead. You contact the ship and order the beast to be beamed aboard. It will certainly provide a few good meals for the crew. You may now either start gathering vegetation for food (turn to 236) or go off in search of other animals to hunt (turn to 173).

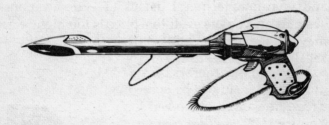

4

The child pulls you off into a building, where several other children are sitting. They squeal excitedly as you enter. Leaving you to talk with them, your guide runs off into another room and returns with another child, who introduces himself as Luff. You explain you are surprised that a child so young was able to contact your ship, and he relates the strange ways of the Terryals.

Apparently, children run the world of Terryal. They are born with abnormal intelligence and abilities and are placed in high positions immediately after birth. As they grow older, they rapidly become senile and incapable of performing their jobs, and then they are replaced by youngsters.

5

You explain your plight to Luff, who listens sympathetically. He may be able to help you in your search for a passage to your own universe. If you wish to follow up this option, turn to 148. He also explains that their medicine is very advanced and he may be able to restore your crew to full strength. If you would prefer this option, turn to 85. However, he asks that in exchange for help or medical treatment, you will have to take him aboard your ship and give him technical details of your weapons systems and defences. If this price is too high, you may decline his offer and return to the ship (turn to 120).

5

M'k Mal declares that you are trespassing in Confederation territory and claims you as a prisoner. He instructs you to follow his ship to a nearby starbase. If you will accompany him, turn to 15. If you refuse to be captured, turn to 143.

6

You set course and arrive at the black hole, dropping out of warp speed some distance from it. Carefully planning your angle of entry and your velocity, you head into the dark void. You feel the ship being taken by the immense gravitational force and order all crew to strap themselves in. Suddenly the ship lurches forwards and begins to speed up. The G-force is so strong that you, along with the rest of the crew, pass out. Turn to **339**.

7

Your MO is unable to make much of the anatomy of the aliens and thus is unable to do much without the use of her lab on the ship. Some of the illnesses, however, seem similar to those on Earth and suggestions can be made on basic medical care. Turn to **210**.

8

You walk up to the entrance door as if to climb into the vehicle. As you pass by the aliens, you signal to the others and the three of you spring on them. This proves to be a rather fruitless exercise, as the three creatures are immensely strong. They fling you to the ground, but as you fall, you manage to grab the helmet off one of the aliens. It stops dead in its tracks in a very artificial pose, as if some switch had suddenly turned it off. The leader grabs the helmet and replaces it on his colleague who instantly springs back to life. You realize you will be no match for the creatures and climb into their vehicle as they have ordered.

But your discovery may prove a useful clue in helping to escape from these PCs, as they call themselves. If you proceed along certain ways, you will be called upon to make a SKILL roll. Your knowledge makes it likely that you will make the right move. You may deduct 2 from your roll when rolling against SKILL which is marked SKILL** (this will make more sense at the time). Turn to **317**.

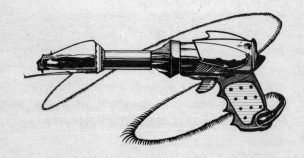

9

Your Science Officer has no suggestions. You must turn either to Commander Domm (turn to **221**) or to the ship's computer (turn to **299**).

10

Roll two dice. If the number rolled equals or exceeds your LUCK score, turn to **123**. If the number is less than your LUCK score, turn to **154**.

11

Back on the bridge, you set your course. Ahead of you are two planets. You may head for either a large red planet (turn to **329**), a blue planet (turn to **2**) or a small, fast-moving spot which shows signs of life (turn to **92**).

12

The guards find your story highly implausible. Cutting you off in mid-sentence, they briskly shove you out into the corridor. Turn to **78**.

13

You land on the planet and look around. A thunderstorm is raging around you and it is pouring with rain. You are standing on rocky ground about a hundred metres from what appears to be a village of some kind. Three aliens, presumably villagers, are shuffling around about halfway to the village but as you appear, they are startled and turn to face you. They are strange, podgy creatures with long necks and stumpy legs. One of the aliens turns and waddles off back to the village at what must be a running pace. The other two are advancing towards you with weapons (long pointed sticks) drawn. Will you:

Wait for them to arrive?	Turn to **115**
Walk towards them to meet them halfway?	Turn to **25**
Make a dash for the village?	Turn to **179**

14

You have an idea: turning up the heat setting on your phaser, you fire at the rock until it glows white hot, hoping that the heat and light will give the ship something to track you by.

You wait, heating the rock until all the energy from your phaser is exhausted. To your great relief, you start to dematerialize and reappear in the ship's Transmatter Unit. Your plan has worked, and you return to the bridge to plot your course. Turn to **27**.

15

You follow the Ganzigites for several hours until a small round object is picked up by your scanners. Ahead of you is a large, wheel-shaped structure, rotating slowly. The Ganzigites announce their arrival. Monitoring their conversation, you learn that this is the spaceport Laur-Jamił. M'k Mal once again contacts you and gives you docking instructions.

You dock the ship and wait while he checks your story. Some time later you see the Ganzigite ship leave dock. Presumably you have either been cleared, forgotten about or ignored. You decide to leave the ship and investigate the spaceport. Turn to **157**.

16

You probe ahead into space with your long-range scanners. On the fringe of your scan radius, to port, is a small star with an orbiting solar system which you may head for (turn to **180**). Otherwise you may increase speed to warp and head off into deep space (turn to **93**).

17

She thanks you profusely. You contact your Engineering Officer on board the ship and explain the situation. He agrees to remain on the planet and help the Macommonians to build their ships. Dilane then offers to take you to the Department of Astronomy. Weapons are not allowed inside the science buildings and you agree to give your phaser to one of the technicians on the door. Turn to **105**.

18

Quickly, the crew seal off the affected area so as to prevent the spread of this unknown killer. No more deaths are reported. Turn to **337**.

19

The wounded creature heaves itself to its feet. It looks at you strangely and cannot understand your concern. Swaying forwards it leads you into the building. Inside is chaos, with broken furniture and scraps of food lying all over the place. The alien slumps down on a bench and concentrates. Slowly, another leg grows out from the previous stump and in no time the wound is repaired! You question the creature, but it appears to have little intelligence. It is a Kroll; it knows nothing of space travel and black holes. It advises you to visit a Timol, who lives several buildings away and is perhaps the most intelligent being in these parts. You thank him and leave. Will you head for the Timol (turn to **231**) or will you investigate the large building at the end of the road (turn to **73**)?

20

The path bends to the right and then forks again. Will you take the left-hand fork (turn to **166**) or the right-hand fork (turn to **113**)?

21

You approach the three men and greet them. They show no interest in you and seem to be arguing about something. Finally they turn to you and in an aggressive tone ask what you want. You relate your story and they are not impressed. Again they ask you what you want. You ask them to take you to their superior (turn to **259**).

22

You, and any crew members with you, spring on the creatures. (These beasts are Squinns.) For hand-to-hand combat rules, turn to **342** but *remember this reference* so that you can return afterwards.

	SKILL	STAMINA
First Squinn	8	16
Second Squinn	7	18
Third Squinn	8	18

If you have other crew members with you, you may order them to attack one of the beasts. The creatures will only attack if they are being attacked themselves. You must kill at least one before you are able to contact the ship, but once one lies dead, you may beam up at any time, taking your prey with you. When you beam up, turn to **311**.

23

Continuing along the ravine, you find only rocky ground. Your portable scanner indicates nothing unusual beneath the surface. Climbing up the slopes you are again hit by the rushing wind, blowing up a dust storm. You decide to beam back up to the ship. Turn to 84.

24

Your Science Officer suggests that since you have your mind inside a Dar-Villian's body, there must be somewhere a Dar-Villian mind inside your body. Perhaps if you repeat the journey through the Transmatter Unit to the same place you will discover the whereabouts of this other body. Do you think this is a good idea? If so, try it by turning to 81. Otherwise you can either ask the alien Commander's opinion (turn to 221) or use the computer for suggestions (turn to 299).

25

They hold their ground and ready their weapons. They shout at you and, through your translator, you hear that they are telling you to remain where you are. You may obey them and wait for them to reach you (turn to 115), or continue. If you wish to continue, turn to 179.

26

In the computer room, the Ganzigite instructs you to leave him alone, return to the bridge and con-

tinue following his own ship. He inserts a small modem into the computer's access port to read its memory and transmit the information back aboard the starcruiser.

From now on, you will be at a disadvantage in any encounters with Ganzigites, as they know your weapons and defences. Deduct 2 points from your ship's WEAPONS STRENGTH and SHIELDS scores in any future battles with this race.

Your Science Officer has informed you of what the alien is doing. Will you take no action until you reach the Ganzig starbase (turn to **202**) or make plans to capture the intruder (turn to **36**)?

27

You scan space around you. Ahead is a greeny-grey planet which you will reach in a few hours. You can continue on course for this planet (turn to **104**). Otherwise you may head for what seems to be a space station a short distance away (turn to **137**).

28

Pick two crew members from the *Adventure Sheet* to accompany you to the planet surface. You enter the Transmatter Unit and minutes later you materialize in a dense jungle on the planet. As you get your bearings, you hear a sound. In the distance, coming closer, is something large crashing towards you through the undergrowth. Will you instruct your party to hide from it (turn to **184**) or draw their phasers (turn to **156**)?

29

The hover-robot once again contacts its central processor. Again it tells you to follow, but again you refuse. Without warning, a stun ray comes from one of its limbs knocking you, and the others in your party, unconscious to the floor. Each member of your landing party must lose 2 STAMINA points. You awake later in a different room. Turn to 187.

30

Your officer gets to work with his micro-excavator. Speaking to you through the communicator, he announces a substantial deposit; plenty for your ship's requirement. Packing several kilos into a portasack, he leaps from the asteroid and dodges his way back towards the ship. Roll one die. If you roll a 1, turn to 190. Otherwise turn to 165.

31

You contact the ship and instruct them to beam you up. You arrive back in the Transmatter Unit, glad to have left the inferno below. You return to the bridge. Turn to 207.

32

You choose two crew members from the *Adventure Sheet* to join you in beaming down from the Transmatter Unit. You dematerialize and appear again on the surface. Looking around, you find you are in an open-air enclosure of some kind with dome-shaped buildings behind you. The noise of a siren pierces the air and from the dome run three aliens similar to

K'tait with weapons drawn! Will you allow them to approach you to see what they want (turn to **111**) or draw your weapons and fire (turn to **122**)?

33

Roll two dice. If the total rolled is *equal to or less than* your Science Officer's SKILL** score, turn to **332**. If the number rolled is *higher* than your SO's SKILL**, turn to **224**.

34

You approach a medium-sized blue-green planet and take up orbit position. Scanning the planet surface reveals several clusters of intelligent life-forms. You try to contact them but nothing comes up on the radio. Will you beam down on to the planet to investigate (turn to **13**) or leave orbit and continue onwards (turn to **203**)? If you beam down, you may take three crew members from the *Adventure Sheet* with you.

35

Roll two dice. If the number rolled *exceeds* your Science Officer's SKILL, turn to **24**. If the roll *equals or is less than* your SO's SKILL, turn to **9**.

36

With you are your Science, Security and Engineering Officers. You may command any one of these to try to overpower the Ganzigite, or you may tackle him yourself. Decide who will take on the alien and turn to **330**.

37

They stop firing and disarm you. Luckily, their weapons were set only to stun, and any crew members hit by their weapons regain consciousness. The aliens escort you to a detention room and lock you in. Turn to **187**.

38

You set course for the black hole, dropping out of warp speed some distance from it. Carefully planning your angle of entry and velocity, you head into the dark void. You feel the ship being taken by the immense gravitational force and order all crew to strap themselves in. Suddenly the ship lurches and speeds up. The G-force is so strong that you and your crew pass out. Turn to **339**.

39

Dilane requests that, in the interests of security, you beam down alone to the surface of the planet, which you do. You appear inside a large, smooth-walled chamber. A door opens and two Macommonians appear in coloured overalls, followed by Dilane herself. Using some sort of detector devices, the technicians check you for weapons and report your phaser to Dilane. She nods and then asks you what you would like to see. Would you like to:

Speak to the Department of Astronomy about ways to get back home?	Turn to **169**
Ask her to show you the city?	Turn to **218**

40

You instruct your navigation officer to plot a course for the double star and give the order to engage warp drive. The ship speeds towards its destination. Suddenly an excited voice comes through your intercom asking you to go down to the canteen, where there has been a disturbance. Turn to 314.

41

Leaving orbit round Jolsen-3 you search the area for life-supporting planets with your scanners. A small yellow planet is picked up as the nearest. Will you proceed to this planet (turn to 89) or continue into deep space (turn to 253)?

42

The creature settles down; it was apparently just surprised at having been woken from its sleep by complete strangers, and such ugly ones at that! It explains that it is a Timol and seems to be quite a friendly creature. It hops around the room and offers you food and drink, which you politely decline. This planet is a settlement planet, populated by all sorts of different aliens, at first mainly creatures who could not bear their own home planets and those that are highly adventurous. As the planet proved to be a pleasant place to live, with a gentle climate, it was not long before word spread throughout the galaxy of this 'promised land' of freedom and equality, attracting many more settlers. The problem was that no one was allowed to assume a position of responsibility – everyone was entirely equal. The result is that, after many years of settlement, the place is in utter chaos. Its inhabitants have not even decided on a name for the planet!

You explain your own predicament to the Timol – how you are lost in a universe parallel to your own. The creature knows little about astronomy and interstellar travel, but suggests you head for the planet Culematter, as its civilization is very advanced. You thank him for his information and leave. You may, if you wish, head for the main building at the end of the road (turn to 73) or you may return to the ship to travel onwards (turn to 290).

43

As the guards enter the room to take the aliens to their Qualk Test, you spring on them. In the battle, the guards may use their nerve sticks. Each time one of your landing party is hit by a guard, throw one die. If you roll a 4, 5 or 6 the hit is with a nerve stick, which will do 4 STAMINA points of damage instead of the normal 2 (a roll of 1, 2 or 3 means normal damage only). For hand-to-hand combat rules turn to **342**, but *remember this reference* so that you can return afterwards.

	SKILL	STAMINA
First guard	8	7
Second guard	7	7
Third guard	8	7

If you defeat the guards, turn to **301**. If you choose to surrender during the fight, turn to **239**.

44

Approaching the purple star, your scanners indicate that the second planet has an atmosphere ideal for life. You drop into orbit around this planet and scan the surface. There are strong indications of intelligent activity. Indeed, it is likely that the planet's civilization is further advanced than your own. You may either beam down to the planet (turn to **171**) or press onwards (turn to **250**).

45

Adjusting the heat setting on your phaser, you fire a beam along the ground, making a circle around yourself. To your relief, the pressure on your leg eases and you are now able to rip the vines from you. However, the drain on your phaser's energy has been severe and you will not be able to use it until you have recharged it on the ship. You may either return to the ship (turn to 311), or continue looking for animals to hunt for food (turn to 173). Whatever you choose, you have already cut down a fair quantity of vegetation and you have this beamed back aboard.

46

Your Medical Officer comes up with a possible antidote and injects herself. She goes down to the docking bay without an EVA suit and waits. An hour later, she has still shown no signs of illness. The antidote has worked! All crew report to the Medical Section for treatment. Turn to 11.

47

Nearing the centre of the cluster, your officer darts about avoiding the asteroids which constantly flash past. Occasionally one will hit another and they will fly off in different directions, sometimes causing a sort of chain reaction. Using a portable scanner, your officer locates four asteroids all bearing dilibrium ore. Which will he choose?

First asteroid	Turn to 30
Second asteroid	Turn to 96
Third asteroid	Turn to 217
Fourth asteroid	Turn to 295

48

Your senior officer flicks his communicator and instructs the ship to beam the crew members, Commander Domm and you back aboard. On the ship, your Science Officer runs an analysis of the situation through the ship's computer. It indicates that you were beamed down to the exact coordinates of one of the Dar-Villian guards and so your body appeared inside his.

You must now decide how you will separate yourself. Will you:

Ask your Science Officer for his opinion?	Turn to 35
Ask your ship's computer for advice?	Turn to 299
Ask the Dar-Villian Commander for any ideas?	Turn to 221

49

You wait for an opportunity and then spring on a guard. It is extremely strong and you are no match for it alone. But if there are two or three of you, and you all fight together, you may overpower it. For hand-to-hand combat rules turn to **342**, but *remember this reference* so that you can return afterwards.

The alien will attack twice in a combat round (so you must roll twice for its *Attack Strength*) and each attack will be directed against whichever of you has the highest STAMINA score (toss a coin if two are equal).

Alien guard   SKILL 11   STAMINA 14

If you reduce the creature's STAMINA to 5, you are able to knock its helmet off, which disables it. If you do this, turn to **147**. If at any time the fight is going badly and you would rather give up the struggle, turn to **309**.

50

Any of the following may be offered to pay your docking fees, as all are valuable to the spaceport: yellow mineral powder, malinite or fluorescent green metal. If you have any of these, you may dock (turn to **157**). Otherwise you will have to bargain with them (turn to **294**).

51

The ship's computer has no information on the Imperial Ganzig Confederation. Impatient at your delay, the starcruiser fires a carefully placed shot across your bows; it is absorbed by your shields –

but at a cost of 2 SHIELD points (cross these off on your *Adventure Sheet*). Will you:

Reply to Commander M'k Tel's
request?   Turn to **281**
Return his fire?   Turn to **135**

52

As you approach the spaceport, you receive a confused message warning you not to dock. You try again to contact the spaceport, but receive no reply. Will you risk continuing with your plan and docking (turn to **193**) or turn away and resume your previous course (turn to **109**)?

53

As you pass through the frame you fall forwards. You panic, but then you realize that you are not really falling, but rather floating, downwards through empty space. Gradually your surroundings become lighter and you can see that you are coming to a sort of pathway, seemingly made of a non-material energy. As you alight on it you look around. The path twists and turns, forks and converges ahead of you like a spider's web set in a black void. The path appears to be able to support your weight, but all around is empty blackness. Cautiously, you proceed along the path, feeling your way with your feet.

Ahead of you the path forks. Will you take the left-hand fork (turn to **293**) or the right-hand fork (turn to **312**)?

You try to continue the conversation but you succeed only in making him angrier. He calls out to his companions and two Terryals enter the room with weapons drawn. 'See them off!' he shouts and the two aim their weapons. The old man also draws a weapon and the three aliens fire at you. Turn to **343** for rules on phaser combat but *remember this reference* so that you can return afterwards. The Terryals fire first.

	SKILL
Old man	6
First Terryal	7
Second Terryal	5

If you survive the battle, you may beam back aboard the ship together with any surviving crew members. Turn to **120**.

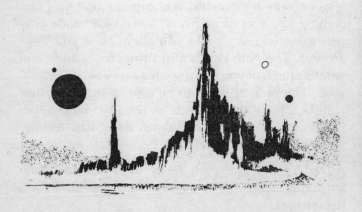

55

You enter the building and look around. It appears to be a library of some sort. You notice on the entrance desk a type of newspaper and take it with you; perhaps it will give you some sort of clue as to why this whole city seems to be deserted. Luckily, the library is computer controlled. You switch on a console and after some whirring sounds, a voice comes back: 'Good afternoon, reader. What subject will it be today?' First of all you ask for local history, but the most recent entry appears to be some time ago when this city was bustling with life.

One of your crew members rushes over. 'Captain,' he says, 'I've just been looking at the astronomy files. There is a black hole which they think may be a space warp. It is in Sector 288!' This news is indeed exciting and you instruct the ship to beam you back aboard to check this location. Turn to **130**.

56

The planet is black and barren with a rough, rocky surface. You explore for half an hour and then decide to beam back to the ship as your air will shortly run out. Trying your communicator, you are horrified to find that you cannot reach the ship! Your Science Officer suggests that this may be because of the magnetic rocks on the planet, jamming your signal. He considers the problem for some time and comes up with an idea. Throw two dice. If the number rolled *equals or is lower than* his SKILL score, turn to **117**; if it *exceeds* his SKILL, turn to **313**.

57

You select two crew members from the *Adventure Sheet* to accompany you to the planet. As you materialize on its surface, you are greeted by K'tait. He invites you into his office and tells you more about the planet. You explain you feel that the only way back to your own universe is to travel back through a black hole, and ask whether anyone on the planet is likely to be able to help. He thinks this likely. A bleeper on his desk summons him to 'the arena'. He makes his apologies and leaves. You await his return. Turn to **287**.

58

You try another all-frequency message, but get no reply. Another blast rocks the ship. Roll two dice. A roll *equal to or lower than* your SHIELDS score does 1 point of SHIELDS damage. A roll *higher* than your SHIELDS score does 2 points, and a double 6 does 5 points of SHIELDS damage. You issue the battle stations order. Turn to **235**.

59

You drop out of warp drive a safe distance from the black hole. Your Science Officer works out your optimum course on the ship's computer. As you advance you can feel the immense gravitational pull of the collapsed star. You allow the ship to be sucked in while the crew strap themselves in. The ship is ripped forwards into the void and all personnel pass out. Turn to **339**.

60

You approach the small cluster. A message from your catering officer comes through your intercom. 'Captain,' he reports, 'I've just discovered a malfunction in one of our freezers. We have lost a good deal of food. What we have left will last the crew for no more than forty-eight hours!' You agree that you must now find supplies for the ship.

Scanning the cluster ahead you locate two planets of suitable temperatures and gravities to sustain life; one is green in colour, the other blue. Will you investigate the green planet (turn to **136**) or the blue one (turn to **260**)?

61

Set your phasers and fire. Turn to **343** for rules for phaser fire. Each member of your party may fire once at the guard. If your phasers are set to *stun*, add 2 points to each dice roll as the guard is armoured (do not make this deduction if your phasers are set to *kill*). If you hit the guard, turn to **244**. If you all miss, turn to **237**.

62

You set course and arrive at the black hole, dropping out of warp speed some distance from it. Carefully planning your angle of entry and velocity, you head into the dark void. You feel the ship being taken by the immense gravitational force and order all crew to strap themselves in. Suddenly the ship lurches forwards and begins to speed up. The G-force is so strong that you, along with the rest of the crew, pass out. Turn to **339**.

63

The guards collect themselves and train their weapons on you. Keeping you in front, they march you down the corridor and into an elevator. After several minutes' travel you arrive at the Detention Centre where you are thrown into detention rooms. Unknown to you, the Dar-Villians are at a loss to decide exactly how to deal with your problem. They eventually decide the easiest solution to the problem is to get rid of it. A gas seeps into the room through the air vent and you drift into an unconsciousness from which you will not awake . . .

64

The Contests are organized annually on Malini to provide amusement for the mine-workers. They are an assortment of athletic events testing all aspects of skill and endurance. The aliens you are in with are entered in the Qualk Test. Qualks are semi-intelligent, rapid-flying beasts with long, razor-sharp beaks. On Malini they are considered dangerous pests. Your room-mates will be armed with phasers and will try their luck against a quazzen (thirty to forty) of Qualks. Winning means both freedom and generous rewards of malinite.

You may either wait to see what game you are to be entered in (turn to 239) or plot an escape (turn to 43).

65

You allow the crew two hours' leave at the spaceport to relax. Most of the crew, along with you and your officers, head for the games room and bar.

The bar is a rather unsavoury place, dark and smoky. A number of strange alien types are drinking colourful drinks and they eye you suspiciously as you enter. You sit at a corner table after ordering your drinks. Next to you is a group of identical creatures, all with dark, warty skin and long noses. One of them bumps into you and grunts menacingly. Your officers rise to your defence. One thing leads to another and before you can stop it, tempers flare and a fight breaks out.

Each of the officers and Security Guards on your *Adventure Sheet* takes on one of the aliens and you must fight each combat to the death. For hand-to-hand combat rules, turn to **342** but *remember this reference* so that you can return afterwards. Each of the aliens is identical:

Bar creatures   SKILL 7   STAMINA 6

When all the fights are concluded, you (if you are still alive) give the order to return to the ship immediately. Turn to **242**.

66

Landing the recon plane, the party make their way to the briefing room to report to you. As they relate their findings, you are interrupted suddenly with an urgent message: 'Captain! We have lost three of our engineering personnel who were involved with docking the recon plane. They are all dead!' What will be your first command?

Put the landing party into
quarantine in the Medical
Section   Turn to **306**
Seal off the docking bay   Turn to **18**
Jettison the recon plane   Turn to **201**

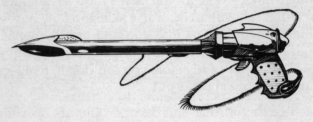

67
You try your communicator, but can hear only static. Something in the building is jamming your signal. However, as you try the controls, you notice something strange. All the aliens you can see are motionless, like statues. You have discovered what may be a way to escape. You turn off your communicator and the aliens come back to life. Turn to **215**.

68
Conditions are very primitive. Your MO notices that many of the aliens have a fever and tries a drug which appears to bring their fever down. The aliens are grateful for your help. Turn to **210**.

69

You are now faced with a problem. You may continue at warp speed and hope your supply of dilibrium lasts until you reach your destination (turn to **10**) or you may hook in an auxiliary power source, which will drain energy from one of your other functions (turn to **323**). Which will you choose?

70

Your Engineering Officer disappears to his lab and sets to work. An hour later he bleeps you. He has tried different types of screening devices in the filter but cannot make one work. You will have to take advice either from your Science Officer (turn to **35**) or from the alien Commander (turn to **221**).

71

With weapons drawn, you watch the creatures carefully. There is a short exchange of calls and your previous 'shelter' crashes off through the jungle. You now stand facing the new arrival. Turn to **156**.

72

The crowd roars as the robot topples and crashes to the ground. You are led away to meet the senior executive of the mining organization who presents you with the customary prize: freedom and a handsome quantity of malinite. You mention your mission and your desire to find a way back to your own universe. He nods and asks you to follow him to the Astronautical Headquarters. Turn to **280**.

73

Steps lead up to the large building. An inscription on the door indicates that it is a building of some importance. You knock but there is no reply, although you can hear excited chatter coming from within. You try the door, it opens and you step into a large entrance hallway. Several pairs of aliens of a variety of shapes and sizes cross the corridor in front of you, travelling purposefully from room to room and arguing excitedly with each other. A mysterious creature, dressed in shabby blue robes, notices you and shuffles over. Its face cannot be seen but its eyes shine bright blue at you. It speaks and your translator interprets: 'Ah, you look interesting. Where do you think the new medicine house should go?' You explain that you are new to these parts and that you would like to meet some person of authority. The alien laughs: 'No one has authority here, my friend. We are all equal! Come, let me show you round.' He offers to take you:

To the main meeting hall	Turn to **161**
On a general tour	Turn to **103**

74

The Service Robot leads you to a waiting room. After several minutes you are shown into a plush office with polished metal walls. Behind a desk standing before a large window looking out into space sits a large creature. It has a large head and torso and is shaped like an old-fashioned egg-timer.

The alien introduces himself as D'Ouse-E and asks how he may help you. He is apparently the Controller of this spaceport. You explain your position and ask whether he may be able to help you find your way back to your own universe. He asks you to wait while he contacts his Mapping Section. Sitting bolt upright, in a state of meditation, he appears to be contacting someone by telepathy. You wait patiently.

Suddenly he snaps out of his trance. 'I cannot guarantee that this information will help you,' he says, 'but my mapping officer has done some studies on gateways between universes. It seems likely that two universes will touch in the near future – Stardate 77 to be precise – although there is no way of telling whether this is likely to be your own universe. You will be able to transfer only through a black hole, but he cannot be certain which one.' You thank him for his information and return to the ship. Turn to 242.

75

The unconscious captor is taken to the Medical Section where your Medical Officer runs tests. Roll two dice. If the number rolled is *equal to or higher than* your Medical Officer's SKILL score, turn to 90. If the roll is lower than your MO's SKILL, turn to 213. If your Medical Officer has been lost or is the affected crew member, her second-in-charge will run the tests; in this case, deduct 2 from the MO's SKILL as recorded on your *Adventure Sheet*.

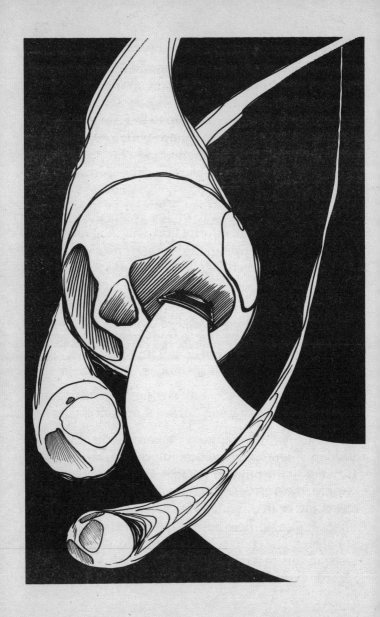

76

You collect the guards' weapons and return to Commander Domm's headquarters. With weapons poised you enter the room. Your senior officer suggests you return to the ship to look for a solution to your problem, taking Domm with you. Turn to 48.

77

The path continues and you soon arrive at another fork. Will you take the left-hand fork (turn to 312) or the right-hand fork (turn to 192)?

78

Under armed guard you are taken to a waiting room and left with several other competitors. Will you ask them more about the Contests (turn to 64) or ask them about how you may escape (turn to 94)?

79

As you approach, you cut engines. Switching to visual on the screen, you can see the small cluster in the distance.

Suddenly your navigation officer wheels round. 'Captain!' he exclaims, 'meteor storm dead ahead. We are moving straight into it!' What will your command be?

Evasive action	Turn to 254
Activate shields	Turn to 283

80

Your officers try their best with the crew, but morale is low. There are reports of two suicides. The Medical Section becomes overloaded with crew suffering from nervous disorders.

Your navigation officer contacts you excitedly. 'Captain!' he exclaims, 'sensors have picked up a black hole 4·2 light years from here!' You decide on an all-or-nothing course and enter warp drive towards it. Turn to **59**.

81

You step into the Transmatter Unit and are beamed down to Dar-Vil. You arrive in the same state. The experiment has not worked. You have yourself beamed up again; you must now either consult the computer (turn to **299**) or ask Domm's advice (turn to **221**).

82

You set course and arrive at the black hole, dropping out of warp speed some distance from it. Carefully planning your angle of entry and your velocity, you head into the dark void. You feel the ship being taken by the immense gravitational force and order all crew to strap themselves in. Suddenly the ship lurches forwards and begins to speed up. The G-force is so strong that you, along with the rest of the crew, pass out. Turn to **339**.

Your Science Officer takes a dump of the weather control program back to the ship to try to analyse it on the ship's computer. It has been written in a strange language, but the computer is able to give some insight into its logic patterns. Your SO alters it slightly and runs the modified program. Within a few moments, the rain dies down. Bran-Sel is delighted and offers to use his computer to search for a suitable black hole to transport you back to your own universe. The computer locates several such black holes; unfortunately it cannot distinguish between them, but it is able to tell you that you will have to travel towards it at warp speed 3 to effect the transfer successfully.

You thank Bran-Sel for his help and beam back aboard the ship. Turn to **203**.

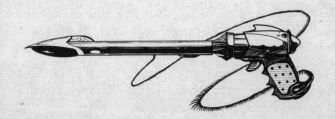

84

Back in the ship you enter your report in the computer and use long-range scanners to probe for your next destination (if you needed dilibrium crystal, the ore you have found is converted in the Engineering Section). Scanners indicate two likely stars ahead with planetary systems in orbit; one a bright purple star and the other a double star. If you wish to head for the former, turn to **270**; to investigate the double star, turn to **40**.

85

Luff calls in one of his medics to accompany you up to the ship, but you must leave your two crew members on the planet as security. You and Ledoux, the medic, beam back aboard the *Traveller*.

Over the next hour, Ledoux treats all the crew members who require medical aid. The two of you then return to the planet where the medic treats you and your two companions. You may restore to their initial values the SKILL and STAMINA scores of all crew members listed on your *Adventure Sheet*. Turn to **229**.

86

You increase speed towards a dull blue planet and start to orbit it. Short-range scanners indicate that it is a life-bearing planet. The most heavily populated area appears to be a city in the centre of a large island. You may beam down into the centre of this city taking any other three crew members from the

Adventure Sheet with you (turn to **209**) or you may leave orbit and continue onwards (turn to **321**).

87

You pause for a moment to see whether the plants will now desist. But the vines entwine themselves round you, pinning your arms against your body. In a panic, you try to wrench yourself free but your struggles are of no avail. You are unable even to contact the ship. The plants tighten their hold around your neck; you are gasping for air, but powerless to stop the plants throttling you. You have ended your days as food for the very plants you thought would feed your crew.

88

The doppelganger transmits a message to the ship, instructing all crew to take twenty-four hours' leave on this planet, 'for it is very hospitable, as friendly as Malthus-4'. Your Science Officer picks up your clue. Malthus-4 is a desolate planet inhabited by an extremely warlike race and used by the Earth as a prison planet. Your Science Officer demands that the Captain return to the ship to give the order in person. The Macommonians cannot allow the doppelganger to be examined closely, so it continues to communicate by radio. Much to the horror of the Macommonians, on being questioned it tells your Science Officer what has happened. Under threat of devastation by the ship's phasers, they agree to release you. You beam up to the ship. Turn to **141**.

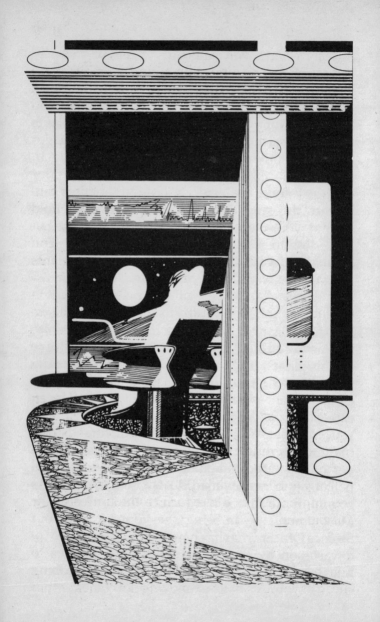

89

You take up orbit position round a small planet circling a large red star. Scanners indicate the planet is probably devoid of life. The surface is hot and volcanic. Will you beam down to explore (turn to 145) or leave (turn to 207)?

90

After extensive analysis, your Medical Officer cannot find any reason why this fit of madness should have occurred. Unable to do any more for the patient, she suggests holding the affected crew member in the brig until you find a cure. Security Guards take him to the detention quarter and lock him in the brig. This crew member will take no further part in this adventure. You return to the bridge. Turn to 336.

91

As you enter, your eyes widen. You are not in the great hall, or perhaps stateroom, you had been expecting, but in a large computer complex. The walls are lined with sophisticated control panels covered in gauges, dials and indicator lights. In the centre of the room, behind a large screen flanked with a number of keyboards, sits a human figure. As you approach, this figure turns round on his chair. Turn to 164.

92

You head out into space, with scanners probing ahead of you. A small fast-moving dot comes within range. As you approach it, you identify it as another ship. You send out an all-frequency radio message and soon an alien face appears on your screen. The face is brown, scaly and somewhat reptilian and introduces itself as Commander M'k Mal of the Imperial Ganzig Confederation. Have you come across the Imperial Ganzig Confederation before? If so, turn to **335**. If not, turn to **5**.

93

You drop out of warp speed near a cluster of stars which looks interesting. You decide to investigate. Turn to **79**.

94

The aliens sharing your room are a quarrelsome bunch, perhaps miners who, tiring of the mines, are hoping to get rich quick, since the prizes for the games in which they are entered are apparently valuable. The chances of escape, you are told, are slim. The anterooms are heavily guarded and the guards are armed with nerve sticks which inflict tremendous pain on their victims. You may either try your luck at whatever contests are in store (turn to **239**) or plot an escape by ambushing the guards as they enter the room (turn to **43**).

You are led away to the Detention Centre. Two new guards who are escorting you are watching your crew more carefully than they are watching you. As you turn a corner in the corridor, you have a chance to grab one of them. But half of you resists this urge and you must fight hard to overcome this resistance. You seize your chance and grapple with one of the guards, but your strength is weakened by your inner conflict.

	SKILL	STAMINA
Your guard	7	6
You	6	7

While you are fighting, your crew are taking on the other guard.

Guard	SKILL 7	STAMINA 7

Turn to 342 for full hand-to-hand combat rules, but *remember this reference* so that you can return afterwards. First you will fight an attack round with your guard, then your crew members will fight an attack round with their guard, and so on. If your crew kill their guard, they will come to your aid. If you kill your guard, you may aid your crew.

If you and your crew defeat the guards, turn to 76. If things are going badly and you wish to stop the fight, turn to 63.

96

Taking a micro-excavating tool from his belt, your officer begins work on the asteroid. The deposit is substantial and he is able to pack several kilos of ore into his portasack. Carefully avoiding the oncoming asteroids, he leaps out towards the ship. Turn to **190**.

97

You continue scanning the surface. It is a high-density planet with a metallic crust. You choose two crew members from the *Adventure Sheet* to accompany you and climb into anti-grav suits in the Trans-matter Unit. Moments later you are on the surface of the planet. Turn to **230**.

98

These offerings have a somewhat synthetic taste and texture, but are not unpleasant, and you begin to talk to the First Officer about your own world, while he tells you about Jolsen-3. A short time later, you begin to feel drowsy, which is very strange as you are not due a rest for several hours. Your eyelids get heavy and you must fight to remain conscious.

Too late you realize that your food was drugged. As you drift into sleep, you hear I-Abail saying to his assistant: 'Let us take our visitor to the portal lab.' Turn to **127**.

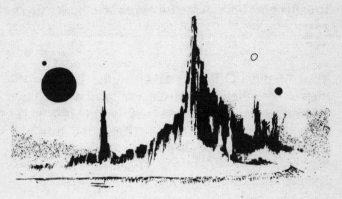

99

You engage the Ganzigite in a conversation and give him a conducted tour of the ship, stalling for time. You show him the cargo hold, shuttle dock, recreation area and science laboratories. In the animal behaviour lab, the alien shrieks as it sees an eagle chained to a perch. You deduce that, on the Ganzigite's world, similar creatures are deadly enemies. Will you:

Ignore the incident and continue the tour via the computer room?	Turn to **26**
Release the eagle?	Turn to **245**
Make use of the distraction to capture the alien?	Turn to **36**

100

The creature seems to consider you for some time, then turns and ambles off into the jungle. You may now either start gathering vegetation for food (turn to **236**) or set off looking for animals to hunt (turn to **173**).

101

Your Medical Officer is taken round some of the huts to see whether anything can be done. Roll two dice and compare the total with your MO's SKILL score. If the roll *equals or exceeds* her SKILL, turn to **7**. If the roll is *lower* than her SKILL, turn to **68**.

102

The guards are a little hesitant, but as the struggling has ceased, they slowly release him. You start to talk to him and as you do so he leaps across the room at you before anyone can hold him back! You struggle together. Have two rounds of combat (turn to **342** for combat rules, but *remember this reference* so that you can return afterwards). Your assailant's frenzied condition gives him extra power – add 3 points to his SKILL. After two rounds of combat, turn to **240**.

103

Your guide, who is called Fioral, shows you from room to room, explaining the planet. 'Our gods are freedom and equality,' says the little creature. 'This is an extremely pleasant planet to live on and it

welcomes settlers of all types. Everyone is entirely equal, whether they have lived here all their lives or have just arrived. Everyone may also do anything they like here – we have no need for laws.' He shows you round the records office, planning area and rooms of state.

On the way back to the debating chamber, you pass the guard room. You ask why, if there are no laws, they have the need for guards. Fioral stops and explains, 'Guards do not guard things, we do not need to protect things. It's just that some members of our community get pleasure out of attacking others and, of course, they are free to do as they wish. But in fairness to the rest of the population, they dress up in uniforms and call themselves guards so as to warn others that they must be on guard when a guard passes. Do you understand?'

While you are considering this, however, three of these guards have left their room and have crept up behind you. They leap on your backs and wrestle with you. Fioral backs away.

	SKILL	STAMINA
First guard	8	10
Second guard	7	9
Third guard	7	10

For full rules for hand-to-hand combat turn to **342**, but *remember this reference* so that you can return here afterwards.

If you defeat all the guards, turn to **150**.

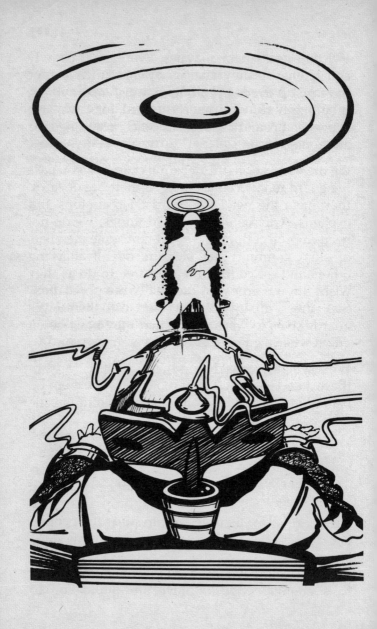

You reduce speed some distance from the planet and take up an orbit position. Scanners indicate the greeny-grey planet supports life and there are positive indications of intelligent beings. If you wish to beam down to the planet, turn to 118. If you will leave orbit and continue your journey, turn to 296.

You hand your phaser to one of the technicians and follow Dilane through the door. In the corridor outside you feel a blow on the back of your head and slump unconscious to the ground.

When you awake, you find that you are strapped into a large metal chair. Probes are attached to your body and in front of you a large scanning device is slowly moving downwards. The scanner is connected to another similar chair and, as you watch, a human outline is taking shape. Slowly the shape forms and you realize what is going on. The Macommonians are making a replica of you!

Dilane enters the room with two other females, apparently of some importance, judging by their tunics. 'Our visitor is awake,' she says. You demand to know what is going on. 'We are not an aggressive race,' she begins, 'but in times of desperation, we must take all steps necessary to save our people. Our planet is being torn apart by the gravitational influences of our two suns. We have less than a year before Macommon will be uninhabitable. We do not have enough ships to move our population to another world. We must claim your starship. As we would be unable to force you to evacuate the ship, we must persuade your crew to beam down by trickery.' Evidently she intends to broadcast a message back to the ship from the counterfeit captain they are making, ordering the entire crew to beam down, leaving the ship for them to take over.

Roll two dice. If the total is equal to or less than your SKILL, turn to 303. If the total exceeds your SKILL, turn to 247.

106

The Service Robot leads you to an office, where you make arrangements to have your ship serviced; you may restore your ship's WEAPONS STRENGTH and SHIELDS scores to their initial levels.

You may now make arrangements for leaving the spaceport. Turn to 242.

107

The feeling soon passes and your MO recovers after a brief rest. Your party then discusses what to do next. Turn to 304.

108

You run off the road and follow him into the building. 'Just in time!' he exclaims. 'You don't want the PCs to find you in the street, do you?' You have no idea what he is talking about. You explain you are not from this planet. He is on his guard. You reassure him that you mean no harm, you just want information which may help you get home, and he calms down. 'You are on the planet Culematter,' he informs you. 'The PCs you have just escaped from are the Population Controllers. On this planet no one dies, but as the population increases, it is necessary to exterminate some of us to make room for others. The PCs have the authority to exterminate anyone they like, within certain quota limits, without reason. They would certainly have killed you had they caught you outside after curfew hours.'

Suddenly the door crashes open and three creatures in armoured uniforms step in. 'I thought I saw them enter this building!' their leader declares. 'Outside!' he orders. Your host protests that you are aliens and did not know about the curfew laws, but the PC leader points a finger and an electric blue ray burns through his chest! You decide it would be prudent to follow the PCs outside. Turn to **140**.

109

You take up orbit position round the large grey planet and scan the surface. There are positive signs of intelligent life and you try an all-frequency radio message. Some time later a message comes through and you transfer it to the screen. A grey-coloured alien with a tiny round mouth and flattened nose appears and introduces himself as K'tait of the Malini Mining Outpost. You introduce yourself and tell him of your mission. You learn that Malini is a mining planet, mining malinite, a valuable mineral ore. He invites you down to the planet and suggests your crew may well be interested in a visit as the 'Contests', sporting events arranged for the entertainment of the miners, are in full swing. He gives you coordinates for beaming down but interference distorts the message and you cannot be certain whether he gave you 223.473.85 or 223.473.83.

You may prefer to ignore this planet and continue on your journey (turn to **320**) or you can try 223.473.85 (turn to **32**) or 223.473.83 (turn to **57**).

110

Your officer swings round and yells loudly as he sees the approaching rock. He leaps to one side, but is not quick enough. The asteroids collide, trapping him between them and ripping his suit open. Exposed to the vacuum of space, he vaporizes instantly, while you can only watch in horror.

You must decide whether to risk sending another officer out for the dilibrium ore (turn to **327**) or to abandon the operation and continue your voyage (turn to **69**).

111

They run up to you and surround you. You explain that you have been invited down by K'tait, but they have never heard of him and grab you, taking your phasers. They seem to be some kind of security guards. They escort you to a detention room and lock you in. Turn to **187**.

112

Flipping your communicator, you instruct the ship to beam the alien back aboard so that your Medical Officer may have a look at him. If your Medical Officer is with you on the planet, she will have to accompany the alien back to the ship and another crew member can come down to replace her. The alien disappears. You prepare to continue, but a message from the ship comes through. Apparently, the alien did not arrive! You confirm that it definitely left the planet. There is little you can do about it now and you leave the problem with your transmatter crew. Turn to **220**.

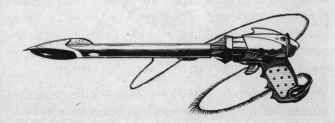

113

You soon arrive at another fork. You may take either the right-hand fork (turn to **166**) or the left-hand fork (turn to **192**).

114

You set course and arrive at the black hole, dropping out of warp speed some distance from it. Carefully planning your angle of entry and velocity, you head into the dark void. You feel the ship being taken by the immense gravitational force and order all crew to strap themselves in. Suddenly the ship lurches forwards and begins to speed up. The G-force is so strong that you, along with the rest of the crew, pass out. Turn to **339**.

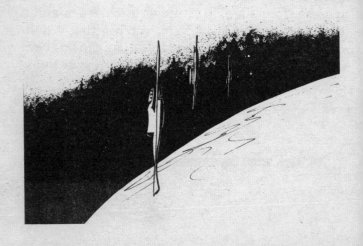

115

Through your translator, you talk to them, explaining your mission. They are suspicious and hold you at bay with their weapons, but agree to take you to the village Elder to talk. Turn to **170**.

116

She understands that you could not do without your Engineering Officer. 'Perhaps,' she says, 'your crew would like to come down to our planet. They would be perfectly safe inside the protection domes and we have excellent medical and recreational facilities here. We are always anxious to meet travellers.' If you would like the crew to relax for some time on Macommon, turn to **286**. Otherwise you may thank Dilane, return to the ship and plot your next voyage (turn to **141**).

117

He suggests you concentrate your phasers on a nearby rock. Soon the rock is white hot and he is hoping that this light and heat will be picked up by the ship. Your oxygen is getting dangerously low but all you can do is wait. A few moments later, your Science Officer dematerializes and you breathe a sigh of relief as you also disappear. Your party reappears in the Transmatter Unit. You climb out of your grav-suit and make your way back to the bridge. Turn to **27**.

Before beaming down, you try to establish radio contact with the planet to see whether you are welcome. After some moments you receive a message and you switch it to the screen. A face appears and asks you to identify yourself. The alien is thin and white skinned, with a long, bone-shaped face. You explain who you are and ask whether you may beam down to meet him. He introduces himself as Luff, of the planet Terryal-6 and gives you permission to beam down.

You go to the Transmatter Unit, selecting two crew members from the *Adventure Sheet* to go down to the planet with you. You beam down to coordinates in the vicinity of the radio transmission and appear moments later on the planet. Looking around you, you find that you are not actually *on* the planet. You are near the edge of a vast floating plane, hovering in the air above the land. This plane is supporting a number of tall buildings. Some distance below, on the ground, you can see groups of what must be factories of some kind, surrounded by agricultural farmland. You are on an island, floating high in the sky!

In front of you is a group of three of the lean Terryals, with a couple of their children. One of the children runs over to you, grabbing your hand and pulling you off in another direction. Will you follow this child (turn to 4) or make your way over to the adults (turn to 21)?

119

As the red light becomes brighter and the humming pitch increases, you begin to feel warm. Suddenly, your Engineering Officer, who has been watching the indicators on the device's control panel, hits a red button. He apologizes, explaining that the screening element seems to have overheated and he cannot risk sending you through the filter. He will return to his lab to work on another screen. Turn to **70**.

120

Back aboard the ship you give instructions to prepare to leave orbit and head immediately for the bridge. Turn to **296**.

121

You make your request, but the alien merely shoves you forwards. 'This is not possible,' it replies. 'You are to be taken to the extermination chamber.' You may try to overpower it while you are alone (turn to **297**) or you may follow it to see what will happen to you next (turn to **215**).

122

As you go for your phasers, they fire at you. You must resolve this phaser shootout but, as their weapons were already drawn, they fire first at you:

	SKILL
First Malinian	8
Second Malinian	7
Third Malinian	9

For phaser combat rules, turn to 343 but *remember this reference* so that you can return afterwards. During the first round of combat, you are some distance from your opponents, so you and the Malinians must add 3 points to your dice rolls. During the second round, you are closer, so you add only 2 points to your dice rolls. During the third round you add 1 point and from then onwards you fight as normal.

If you wish to surrender to them at any time, turn to 37. If you stun or kill the Malinians, turn to 225.

123

Your Engineering Officer protests loudly, but you order him to continue at your present speed. The warning indicator begins to flash as it enters overload. Will you stick to your decision (turn to 278) or slow down and hook up an alternative energy source (turn to 323)?

124

Your Science Officer suggests that you all return to the ship to run a situation analysis through the ship's computer. Roll 2 dice. If the number rolled *equals or exceeds* your Science Officer's SKILL, turn to **251**. If the number is *less* than his SKILL, turn to **48**.

125

You cautiously continue down the road with phasers set on *stun*. You begin to hear quiet chatter coming from one or two of the buildings and a peculiar face appears at a window. You are unsure whether the creature has intelligence or not and, as you debate whether to approach that building, a noise behind you makes you all swing round.

A tall, spindly creature some three metres high has approached you. It has six spider-like legs and its long neck holds its head well above you. It speaks to you and your translators give its message as 'Hello, friends. You are not at all welcome in the Avenue of the Committee. You must leave immediately. Can I offer you warmth and a drink?' This strange message leaves you puzzled. You announce who you are, where you are from, and insist that you mean no harm. The alien is not in the least bit interested and has begun to shiver. Will you accept its hospitality (turn to **177**) or leave it and head for one of the other buildings (turn to **231**)?

You switch to warp drive and head towards the red planet. As you reduce from warp speed, you approach a small, grey planet. Will you investigate this (turn to **261**) or will you continue towards your original destination (turn to **329**)?

You awake and try to move. You struggle, but some invisible force holds your limbs. You are in a clean, white room with various machines and computer terminals on hover-tables around the walls. I-Abail stands before you. 'Stranger,' he begins, 'you have a privileged opportunity to aid our technological development. Our technicians have developed a space–time portal which acts as a doorway between our universe and your own. We have chosen you as our first experimental subject!' He points to one corner of the room, where a free-standing frame, something like a door frame, stands. Looking through the frame you can see nothing. Two technicians pull you to your feet and hold you in front of the frame. Another presses a button on a small gadget and, with a faint buzz, your hands and feet are free. You try to break the grip of your captors, but as you do so, they push you forwards through the frame. Turn to **53**.

128

The medical team arrives and prepares to administer a sedative. As they approach the prisoner, he lashes out and cracks one of the guards a nasty blow across the forehead. Throw one die. If you throw a 5 or 6, this is one of the Security Guards on your *Adventure Sheet* and you must deduct 3 points from his STAMINA (toss a coin to decide which guard is hit if there is a choice of two). If you throw 1, 2, 3 or 4, you do not have to deduct anything as this was not one of your named Security Guards. After this incident, the medical team manage to administer the drug and the enraged captive slumps to the floor, unconscious. Turn to 75.

129

Your MO comes up with a possible antidote and tries it out on herself, entering the affected area without an EVA suit. Watching her on a monitor screen, you see her enter the docking bay. Moments later, she falls to her knees! Her antidote has not been successful and you have lost your MO. Turn to 284.

130

Back on board you announce your news to the crew. As the navigation officer sets the course, you remember the newspaper and pass it on to the language lab for analysis. You may set your course either for a purple star just within long-range scanner range (turn to 233) or a small cluster of stars some 2·3 light years off to starboard (turn to 292).

131

For rules of phaser fire, turn to **343** – but *remember this reference* so that you can return afterwards.

	SKILL
First guard	7
Second guard	6
Third guard	7

Your crew may aim at any of the guards and you must decide who they fire at in each round by throwing dice. The distance between you and the guards is considerable, so everyone will add one point to their dice roll, but the guards must add an extra point because you are hiding in the shadows. If you overcome the guards you may enter the keep. Turn to **91**.

132

You set transmatter coordinates for navy headquarters as instructed by Commander Domm. Your party dematerializes in the ship and rematerializes again on the planet. You look around your new surroundings to find you are in a military reconnaissance room of some sort. Armed guards stand by the door. In front of you stands Commander Domm. Your crew are also surveying the room, but they seem to be searching for something. You announce your introduction to the Dar-Villians and everyone in the room stares at you in disbelief! Your own crew are looking at you with astonished expressions on their faces! You feel a little strange but cannot understand their reaction – until you look down at yourself. Your body is that of a Dar-Villian! You are tall and thick-set, and in full military dress. Do you have your Science Officer with you? If so, turn to **289**. If not, turn to **189**.

133

Resuming orbital position, you scan the planet again. Although readings are still puzzling, you cannot find positive signs of life. If your ship is still short of dilibrium crystal you must beam down to the surface to search for deposits (turn to **285**). Otherwise you may beam down to have a look round anyway (turn to **264**) or leave orbit and head onwards (turn to **198**).

134

K'tait apologizes profusely for the confusion. He offers to provide 'the finest view in the house' if you wish to watch the Contests (turn to **310**), or you may beam back to the ship (turn to **320**).

135

Both ships open fire – this will be a battle to the death. Turn to **341** for the rules for ship combat. But *remember this reference*. Once you have read through the rules return here and fight the battle.

Alien ship   WEAPONS STRENGTH 9   SHIELDS 12

If you defeat the starcruiser, turn to **16**.

136

You take up orbit position round the green planet. Scanning the surface you find an abundance of vegetation and animal life, but there are no signs of intelligent inhabitants. Do you wish to beam down? If so, turn to **28**. Otherwise you may leave orbit and head for the blue planet (turn to **260**).

137

You slow down as you approach a large wheel-shaped structure, rotating slowly in space. Making radio contact, you learn it is the spaceport Laur-Jamil. Your ship is welcome to dock and there are facilities for repairing ships, but payment must be made in a currency you have never heard of. Have you picked up anything during your travels which you may be able to use to pay? If so, turn to **50**. If not, you may attempt to bargain with them (turn to **294**) or you may decide not to bother and continue your journey (turn to **324**).

138

You set your course and arrive at the black hole, dropping out of warp speed some distance from it. Carefully planning your angle of entry and your velocity, you head into the dark void. You feel the ship being taken by the immense gravitational force and order all crew to strap themselves in. Suddenly the ship lurches forward and begins to speed up. The G-force is so strong that you, along with the rest of the crew, pass out. Turn to **340**.

139

Your Engineering Officer sets to work. It will take his department some time to rig up a genetic filter. Two hours later he bleeps you to tell you the device is ready for testing. You make your way to his lab to try it out. Inside the lab stands an M-shaped machine positioned over three mattresses. You lie down on the middle mattress and the filter is turned on. Above you, a red light glows and a dull humming noise increases in pitch. Roll two dice. If the number is *equal to or higher than* your LUCK score, turn to **181**. If the number is *lower* than your LUCK score, turn to **119**.

140

You explain that you are from another planet and therefore know nothing of their curfew laws. 'It is illegal to be outside after curfew,' says their leader. 'The penalty is extermination. Enter this vehicle.' Will you enter as they wish (turn to 317), draw your phasers and fire (turn to 206) or pretend to comply with their wishes and take them by surprise (turn to 8)?

141

You prepare to leave orbit. You may head onwards either towards a purple star (turn to 44) or into deep space towards the source of a weak radio signal you are receiving coming from a planet several light years away (turn to 34)?

142

You increase speed towards your destination. Suddenly a red light appears on your control panel. You hit your communicator switch and contact the Engineering Section. 'We'll have to cut speed, Captain,' cries your Engineering Officer. 'The reactor must have been damaged more than I thought. I can't hold her!' You ask what exactly the problem is and learn that your supplies of dilibrium crystal are almost exhausted.

Dilibrium crystal is a naturally occurring mineral common throughout your own galaxy. The raw material can be mined and the ship is equipped with a processing plant to convert it to nuclear fuel. You must begin searching for the mineral straight away, for without dilibrium your ship will be unable to travel. You may either continue as you are, travelling towards the barren system (turn to **69**) or you may investigate a small asteroid cluster you are just passing (turn to **226**).

143

The Ganzigites warn you that refusal to comply with their orders will force them to open fire. You may either decide against a battle and let M'k Mal take you to his starbase (turn to **15**), or order your crew to battle stations and attack:

Alien ship   WEAPONS STRENGTH 8   SHIELDS 12

For ship-to-ship combat rules, turn to **341** but *remember this reference* so that you can return afterwards. If you defeat the Ganzigites, turn to **185**.

144

He is somewhat offended but nevertheless continues the conversation. He offers to take you on a tour of his capital and you agree. To start with he takes you to the Tech Centre, explaining that you may be interested in seeing some of their recent areas of development in technology. Leaving his office, you stand on a moving conveyor belt which takes you on a long trip through tubes and tunnels. Finally you step off outside a door to the portal lab. Inside, this lab is a clean, white room with various machines and computer terminals on hover-tables around the walls.

'In this lab,' explains I-Abail, 'our technicians have developed a space–time portal which opens a doorway between our universe and your own. However, it has yet to be tested. We can offer you the opportunity of being the first subject, and you may find that this is a way of returning to your own universe.' He points towards a structure in one corner of the room which resembles a large door frame. Will you accept his offer and pass through the portal (turn to **158**) or is this a risk you would prefer not to take (turn to **178**)?

145

You may choose two crew members from the *Adventure Sheet* to accompany you down to the planet's surface and head for the Transmatter Unit. You leave the ship and reappear on the surface of the planet. The heat is tremendous and the cooling systems within your EVA suits must work at maximum. The surface of the planet is volcanic and small eruptions in the ground around you spray out molten lava. Will you:

Scan for signs of life?	Turn to **272**
Look more closely at an erupting volcano near by?	Turn to **159**
Return to the ship?	Turn to **31**

146

With proper treatment in the Medical Section, your MO recovers swiftly. You decide not to risk the health of the crew on this planet and discuss your future course with the navigation crew. Turn to **203**.

147

When its helmet is knocked off, the alien stops dead in its tracks as if frozen in time. However, the scuffle has attracted the attention of more guards and they are now on top of you. You cannot take them all on. Turn to **309**.

148

You follow him through several buildings into an observatory. He has words with another child, who is operating a large telescope. The second child then questions you about your arrival. Sitting down at a desk, he talks into a computer terminal and some moments later, information is displayed on the screen. Turning to you, he reports that he cannot be sure of the location of the black hole you seek, but he believes that your two universes will coincide at Stardate 21. You thank him for his help and return with Luff to the meeting room. Turn to **229**.

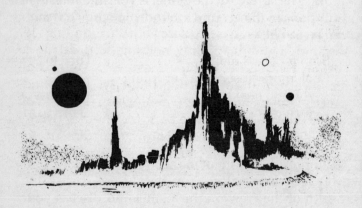

149

You struggle for command of your own voice. You concentrate hard and, to your relief, you are able to express your wishes. The most senior officer in the landing party speaks to the Dar-Villian Commander and he agrees to accompany you back to the ship. Turn to 48.

150

Fioral steps back out of the shadows and approaches you. He seems not to be in the least bit surprised by the scuffle. You ask why the guards attacked. 'Oh, for no reason,' he says. 'They are free to do anything they like.' You may now ask to be shown either the debating chamber (turn to 161) or the travel and maps room (turn to 194), or you can leave the building and beam back to the ship (turn to 290).

151

You look round and see a barren planet. The surface is flat and black. You explore your surroundings for a short time but, finding nothing, you decide to beam back to the ship. However, your communicator will not function properly. The abundance of magnetic rocks is jamming your signal. You have only enough oxygen left for another twenty minutes on the surface. Throw two dice. If the number rolled *exceeds* your SKILL score, turn to 14. If the number is *equal to or lower than* your SKILL score, turn to 313.

152

You search the nearby area for signs of other Scavengers. In one building you hear sounds and go in to investigate. Tied up in one corner of the building is a female Macommonian, struggling to free herself. You cut her loose. She is overwhelmed with gratitude as, in a few minutes, she was due to be tortured for the amusement of the Scavengers. She is from the domed city and her inquisitiveness led her into the ruins where she was captured by the Scavengers. For saving her life she will serve you and, if you wish, you may recruit her into your security staff. She is a skilled fighter (SKILL 9, STAMINA 12), specializing in hand-to-hand techniques. When rolling two dice to determine her *Attack Strength* in hand-to-hand combat, you will have the option of rolling the two dice again if you would like to try to increase the Macommonian's *Attack Strength* (you must, however, accept the second throw even if it is lower than the first).

You may now beam back up to the ship, taking the Macommonian with you if you wish. Turn to **141** and prepare for your next voyage.

153

He suggests you seal off the docking bay, as it seems apparent that a poison of some kind has been brought back to the ship in the recon plane. No doubt the landing party are not affected as they were wearing EVA (Extra Vehicular Activity) suits. You agree and give the command. You also have the areas of the engineering lab which have been affected sealed off. Turn to **18**.

154

The warning indicator light begins to flash as the power drain becomes critical. Your long-range scanners indicate that the planet is 10·38 minutes' journey away. There is a chance that you will make it before you lose warp power. Turn to **174**.

155

As you suspected, their knowledge of astronomy is virtually non-existent. You wind up your talk and signal the ship to beam you back on board. They are bewildered as you dematerialize in front of them. On board ship you plan your next course. Turn to **203**.

156

Will you set your weapons to *stun* (turn to **328**) or *kill* (turn to **3**), or will you wait to see if the beast leaves you alone (turn to **100**)?

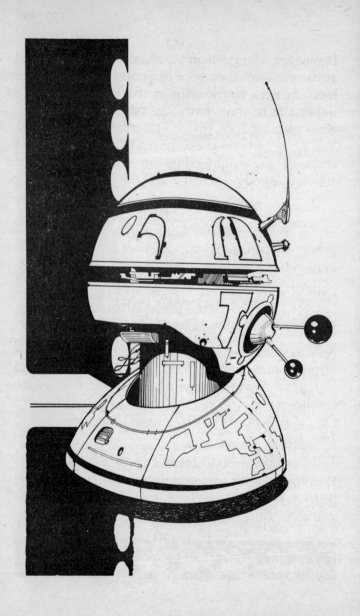

157

Inside the spaceport you follow the corridor until you are approached by a hovering device of some kind. It announces itself as a Service Robot and asks if it may be of assistance. You may ask it:

To take you to someone of authority	Turn to 74
Whether there are recreation facilities here	Turn to 308
How you might go about giving the ship a service overhaul	Turn to 106

158

A technician types commands into a keyboard and, with a buzzing sound, the portal charges up. Looking into it, you can see nothing but blackness. If you wish to change your decision, turn to 178. Otherwise you step forward through the portal. Turn to 53.

159

Your party approaches the rim of a large crater. Looking cautiously over the edge, you peer down into a pool of molten rock. The heat is unbearable. Suddenly the ground behind you ruptures and the rock under your feet crumbles, causing you all to lose your balance.

Roll two dice for each of you in turn and compare the total rolled with your SKILL scores. If any of you roll a number *higher* than your own SKILL scores, the disturbance causes that crew member to fall forwards over the rim to his death in the hellpit below. If *you* die in this way, this adventure is over. If you do not die, you decide to beam back to the ship with any of the crew who have survived. Turn to **31**.

160

You head for the centre of the complex, dodging round the corridors so as to avoid the creatures. You try your communicator several times to reach the ship, but something is jamming the signal. You pass one room in which the walls are covered with electronic equipment. Perhaps this is the transmission room, transmitting the signal which is blocking your own signal to the ship. Two aliens sit inside, but your attempts to contact the ship on your communicator have turned them into statues! Entering the room, you play with the controls until eventually, a signal comes back through your communicator from the ship. You give the order to beam up straight away. It will take several seconds to fix on your exact coordinates and while you wait you remove one of the aliens' helmets. Inside the helmet and the creature's head is a mass of electronic circuitry. You had been captured by androids! You keep the helmet for investigation on the ship and moments later the transmatter beam locks on to take you up. Turn to **269**.

161

You enter the main meeting hall and sit down in a crowded debating chamber, packed with aliens of all shapes and sizes. You ask your host, who is called Fioral, what is going on and he informs you that the debate is to decide where to put a new medicine house – and that it has been going on for the equivalent of a year! As there is no central stage, you ask who is talking. 'Everyone!' says Fioral. 'We believe in equality and everyone has a right to speak.' Apparently debating here is unlike the method used on the Earth. Here everyone collects together and talks in little groups. As debaters move from one group to another, gradually new ideas spread throughout the whole of the chamber, until everyone is thinking along the same lines. At this point, decisions get implemented. You ask whether this takes a long time, and Fioral agrees that it does, but it is the fairest way and prevents a convincing speaker swaying the audience or establishing himself as a leader.

As the debate seems to be getting nowhere, you decide to leave, and Fioral offers to take you to the travel and maps room (turn to **194**). Otherwise you can return to the ship (turn to **290**).

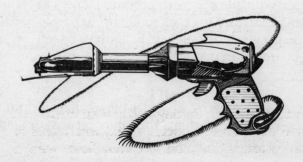

162

At the Commander's instruction, you beam down to the planet's surface. Using communicators, you, your ship and the Dar-Villians focus your transmatters and synchronize timings. Logging into computers, you set the time for simultaneous beamings. At the set time, both transmatter beams focus on you and your body dematerializes. Moments later you appear in the ship's Transmatter Unit – in your own body. The experiment has been a success!

You contact the Commander, who reports that his own officer has likewise reappeared in his Transmatter Unit. You congratulate each other; then you decide to leave orbit and press on. Turn to **316**.

163

You resume your seat on the bridge and plot your course onwards. You have a choice between heading for a purple star with orbiting planets likely to support life (turn to **44**) or making your way towards a small cluster of stars, 2·3 light years off on a starboard course (turn to **79**).

164

'Aha – our intruders!' chuckles the small man sitting at the controls. 'Perhaps they may be able to help with our little problem.'

The man calls himself Bran-Sel. You introduce yourselves and tell him your story. 'I may be able to help,' says Bran-Sel, 'if you are able to help me first.' He goes on to explain that, many years ago, he was an interstellar trader, carrying a cargo of sophisticated planet control computers to Gleena-3 in another sector of the galaxy. His warp drive failed and he was forced into orbit round this planet. He was able to contact Gleena-3 to explain the delay, but they would take no excuses and cancelled the order. Thus he was left with his cargo and no buyer. Facing financial ruin if he returned home, he decided to settle on the planet. Through his advanced knowledge, he was quickly hailed as a sort of god by the inhabitants, who built him a castle in which he could set up his planet control equipment. Since then he has indeed acted as a god and, by his own account, a benevolent one at that. However, some time ago he discovered a malfunction in the weather planning system which meant that he no longer had control over the weather. As the climate was normally very damp, the years of fine weather he had provided for the benefit of the inhabitants' crops had resulted in huge reserves of rain being stored in the planet's clouds. As soon as control was lost, a torrential downpour started.

'If you have a knowledge of planet control systems, and can help me get back control of the weather, I am sure the computer's knowledge of astronomy will be able to help you get back to your own universe,' promises the little man. You decide to call in your Science Officer (if you do not have him with you, you may beam him down from the ship) – turn to 227. If he is dead, you cannot help; you must beam up and leave orbit (turn to 203).

165
Passing through the airlock, your officer hands his portasack to the Engineering Officer who takes the dilibrium ore off to the Engineering Section. One hour later he announces he has enough dilibrium to get the ship under way once more and you may continue on your course. Turn to 248.

166
You arrive at a four-way junction where two paths converge and two further paths branch off to left and right. Will you continue to the left (turn to 293) or to the right (turn to 338)?

167
As the bridge staff collect themselves together, you ask your navigation officer for a report. He replies that you have evaded the meteor storm and are now back on course for the star cluster. Turn to 60.

168
You leave the bridge and await the arrival of the Ganzigite in the Transmatter Unit. Within minutes, a body begins to materialize. The brown, scaly body of a reptilian being takes shape in front of you. You move forward to welcome the new arrival, but the creature snarls at you and draws a weapon.

Through your translator, the Ganzigite commands you to lead him straight to the computer room. Your ship is following the alien starcruiser through space.

You are a little suspicious of this intruder. Will you:

Take him to the computer room
as he wishes? Turn to **26**

Attempt to sidetrack him by
taking him to a lower deck? Turn to **99**

Leap on him and try to overpower
him? Turn to **36**

169

'You will not be allowed to take your weapon into the Department of Astronomy,' she says. Will you hand over your weapon and follow her (turn to **105**) or forget about this visit and ask to see the city (turn to **218**)?

170

As you enter the village area, other aliens shuffle towards you inquisitively. You are marched to a large hut in the centre of the clearing to meet the village Elder. You enter this hut and see a large, somewhat wrinkled alien squatting in a far corner. After you have exchanged introductions you begin to question him. Will you ask him about the planet and its inhabitants (turn to **291**) or do you believe this primitive race can be of little help in your mission but ask anyway about their knowledge of astronomy (turn to **155**)?

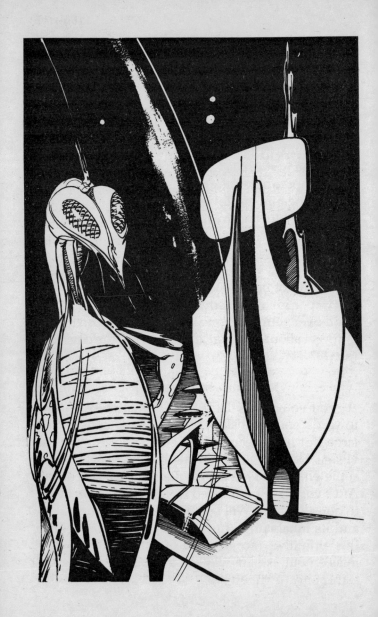

171

You try an all-frequency broadcast several times, but receive no messages in reply. Selecting one Officer and a Security Guard from the *Adventure Sheet*, you enter the Transmatter Unit and beam down to the surface.

You materialize in a deserted street. Tall buildings on one side tower over you, while on the other side of the street the buildings are small; perhaps these are private dwellings. The architecture is alien, but no life of any kind can be seen. In the distance, ahead of you down the road, you can hear a whirring sound; soon you can see a strange vehicle, which seems to be heading towards you. It is a hover-car of some kind and is moving slowly.

As you decide what to do, your translator picks up a sound: 'Over here! Quick!' You look around and see a man-sized, somewhat insect-shaped creature beckoning you into one of the small buildings. Will you follow him in (turn to **108**) or ignore him and wait for the vehicle to approach (turn to **263**)?

172

Your Science Officer reports to you with a suggestion. Throw two dice. If the number rolled is *equal to or less than* your SO's SKILL, turn to **153**. If your roll *exceeds* the SO's SKILL, turn to **255**.

173

Using a portable scanner to locate more animal life, you track down another of the hog-like creatures.

Eventually you come across a clearing where three of these beasts are drinking water. If you are able to use your phaser, turn to **200**. If not, you may tackle them with your bare hands (turn to **22**).

174

Two minutes later, the ship begins to slow down. You contact engineering – your Engineering Officer is distraught. Your dilibrium reserves have been exhausted, and operating on normal power without dilibrium has caused a chain reaction within the ship's energy source. All power, with the exception of battery power, has been lost and there is no way of restoring it. You cannot move and, when battery reserves run out, you will have no energy left even for heat and light. Your ship is a hull, drifting hopelessly in space, and you will never see Earth again . . .

175

Your mind is willing your voice to state your wish to return to the *Traveller*, but your voice is speaking Dar-Villian and is asking Commander Domm to take your crew prisoner and take you to their Intelligence Unit! Turn to **251**.

176

They can find no signs of the pilot. Perhaps he has died or was killed in the crash. An automatic signal, probably a type of Mayday call, is being transmitted by the ship's radio. There being nothing else to see on the planet, your crew return to the recon plane and fly back to the ship. Turn to **66**.

177

The strange creature turns and beckons you to follow. Bobbing up and down on its thin legs it leads you across the road towards a building seemingly made of some kind of clay. Several metres from its door, another alien, this time a small furry one with at least twelve legs, darts from the building next door and stops the tall creature for a brief chat. The two aliens appear to be laughing heartily at some joke – but then the small one springs at the other's legs and bites one off! Your escort slumps to the ground in pain. You are horrified; you may use your phaser to stun the attacker (turn to **307**) or you may rush to the aid of the fallen creature (turn to **19**).

178

I-Abail is again disappointed and tries to persuade you that the risks are minimal. But you are adamant in your decision. 'If that is your choice, so be it!' says the First Officer and, with a nod, he signals the three technicians in the room to advance. It seems he has commanded them to capture you and you will have to fight each of them in turn. For hand-to-hand combat rules, turn to **342** – but *remember this reference* so that you can return here.

	SKILL	STAMINA
First technician	7	7
Second technician	5	6
Third technician	6	6

If you defeat the technicians, turn to **205**. If, however, they inflict 6 STAMINA points' worth of damage on you, turn immediately to **271**.

179

They appear to ready their weapons. Suddenly, the tips of the sticks shoot towards you. Roll two dice for each of your crew members to determine who the aliens are aiming at. The highest dice roll is in the firing line of the first missile and the next highest roll receives the second. Roll two dice for each crew member thus endangered. If the roll exceeds that crew member's SKILL, the missile wounds him seriously. If you have your Medical Officer with you, you will be able to heal anyone seriously wounded. If not, then any wounded crew member will die. After this attack, you decide to hold up your hands and allow them to approach. Turn to **115**.

180

As you approach the small star your scanners pick up two planets in orbit. One is a large red planet, which you may approach by turning to **258**. The other planet is dull blue and you may approach it by turning to **86**.

181

As the pitch increases, you begin to feel uncomfortably warm. The light above you begins to flash and you disappear from your mattress! Consciousness fades and never returns. Genetic filters are only in an elementary stage of development and your Engineering Officer's efforts were not successful. Your body – and that of your Dar-Villian host – have been converted into energy, never to return to the material world . . .

182

As you descend into the ravine, you use your portable scanner to probe the land. Looking downwards you can see what appears to be a stream running along the valley and you climb down to investigate. Your scanner indicates that it is water, but gives a strange reading.

One of your crew members (you choose which one) is a little dry from the dusty air and bends down, taking a drink of the water. You order him to stay away but he has already taken a sip and tells you not to worry, as the stream really is water. On the bank of the river is a natural-looking deposit of a yellow-coloured powder, which your scanner cannot analyse. You may, if you wish, take some of this back to the ship for further analysis. Other than this, the planet seems to be totally barren. If you wish to continue exploring turn to **23**. Otherwise you may beam back up to the ship by turning to **84**.

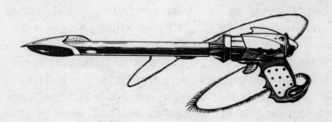

183

The Manslayer Robot has a toughened plasti-metal armour which is resistant to most attacks, although it is vulnerable at certain locations. Each time any of your party attempt to damage the robot, you must roll one die. If you roll a 5 or a 6, you have found a weak spot and may deduct *one* STAMINA point from it. If you roll a 1, 2, 3 or 4, you have hit it on its armour and you cause no damage (i.e. do not deduct STAMINA points).

Manslayer Robot   SKILL 10   STAMINA 4

If you defeat the Manslayer, turn to **72**.

184

The three of you slip back into the undergrowth and wait for whatever it is to appear. The crashing gets louder and louder until a huge beast comes into view. Camouflaged by its green scales, which blend in with the plants of the jungle, this creature resembles a large pig, but with a long, thin snout like that of an anteater. It pauses as if it senses something in the air and comes slowly towards you. Suddenly you feel the foliage moving around you. To your horror, you realize you are hiding right beside another of the beasts, its camouflage so good that you were unable to distinguish it from the surrounding plants! As it moves forwards, a cry comes from one of your landing party and you whirl round to see a great leg, looking more like a tree stump, descending to crush him to death. (Toss a coin to discover which of your two companions has been crushed.) A second leg comes down. Throw one die. If the number is a 1 or 2, your other companion has been crushed. If you roll a 5 or 6, you have been crushed. A 3 or 4 means you are both safe.

Survivors may now draw their phasers and leap out of the way (turn to 71) but if you are dead, this adventure is over.

185
You now have two choices: a large grey planet is some 2·7 light years away (turn to 253 to approach this planet); or you may approach a small planet a short distance ahead at sub-light speed (turn to 89).

186
One of your analysts prepares a paste of the powder and approaches the captive. Although he struggles frantically, the analyst manages to force some of the paste into his mouth. As you wait for something to happen, a remarkable change takes place. The man's face turns from red to blue and his strugglings cease. Eventually he slumps to the floor, unconscious. Medical staff are called in to take him to the Medical Section. When they arrive they check his condition. Turning to you, they announce that it would be a waste of time taking him for treatment – the man is dead. Your powder has poisoned him. Overcome at your blunder, you return to the bridge. Turn to 336.

187
The walls of the room you are in are bare and there appears to be no door in the doorway. But the boot which you toss at the doorway bounces back, confirming your suspicion that you are imprisoned within the room by an invisible energy sheet. Some

time later, guards return with a supervisor who asks whether you are going in for the Contests. Will you tell him that you are (turn to **78**) or try to make him listen to your story (turn to **326**)?

188

The alien injures the eagle, but wails pitifully and begs you to call off the bird, which you do. Apparently eagles are sacred to the Ganzig culture, and injuring them is a mortal sin. You command guards to take the alien to the brig.

Calling up the Ganzigite starcruiser Captain, you relate the incident, threatening the life of your captive if your ship is not freed. The alien Captain agrees to your terms, realizing that he cannot harm a ship carrying sacred animals.

You take your captive to the Transmatter Unit and send him back to his ship. You are now free to leave. Turn to **16**.

189

You wish to return to your ship so that your Science Officer can run an analysis of the situation. However, you are aware of a powerful rebel force within you which you cannot control. Throw two dice and compare the score with your SKILL score. If you roll *higher* than your SKILL, turn to **175**. If you roll *equal to or lower than* your SKILL, turn to **149**.

190

A small asteroid suddenly appears in view in your monitor, travelling at a fair speed. You punch the communicator button to warn your officer, who has not yet seen the object. But to your horror, you are too late! The asteroid crashes into the back of your officer, crushing his jet pack and ripping open the surface of his suit! Helplessly you watch as he vaporizes on the screen.

You have lost a valuable officer. You must now decide whether to risk sending another officer after the crystal ore (turn to **327**) or to abandon the operation and continue towards the planet (turn to **69**).

191

Three technical staff appear through one of the doors and you all beam back to the ship. You allow Luff and his staff access to your computer and take them on a tour of your Engineering Section. After a couple of hours they have all the information they need and you beam them back down to the planet. Turn to **120**.

192

You soon arrive at another fork. You may take either the left-hand fork (turn to 113) or the right-hand fork (turn to 293).

193

You dock at the spaceport and head through the airlock to the command centre. You may take up to three crew members from the *Adventure Sheet* with you. As you walk around the complex you pass creatures of various alien races. Curiously you notice that they all appear to walk with difficulty and shrink away from you as you approach, spluttering and stumbling as if in some sort of daze. At the command centre you meet the port Commandant. He is disheartened by your presence and explains that a resilient strain of micro-organism has infected the spaceport and the infection is widespread. He can send his engineers to attend to your ship but you will have to provide them with EVA (Extra Vehicular Activity) suits and destroy these suits afterwards. You agree. Restore your ship's WEAPONS STRENGTH and SHIELDS scores to their initial levels and leave the spaceport as quickly as possible. Turn to 257.

194

The travel and maps room is in a state of chaos. Books and charts lie all over the floor and the various tables in the room. A small, withered alien with a large head, blue skin and long fingers is asleep in one corner but wakes as you enter. You ask first for maps of the planet but can learn little from them. While you wonder whether any of the star charts will be of use, the little man finds a large map and allows you to study it. Apparently you are in a solar system around the sun Magnus. Apart from this one, there is only one other life-bearing planet in this system, called Trax, orbiting Magnus a little further out. Trax was recently devastated by war and many of its inhabitants left to settle on this planet. The other two nearest planets, although light years away, are Culematter, orbiting a purple sun, and Macommon, orbiting a double star. No black holes are to be found on the chart.

You thank the creature for his help and leave the building, bidding goodbye to Fioral as you leave. Outside you beam back to the ship. Turn to **290**.

195

You follow the hover-robot along a passageway of corridors. Eventually it indicates a room that you should enter. You go into the room and wait, but nothing seems to be happening and no one investigates you. Turn to **187**.

196

You pick your way through the rubble, with Dilane following you nervously. Suddenly a laser blast scorches the wall in front of you. On your left stands a wild-eyed Macommonian – this one a male – with a weapon in his hand. He prepares to fire again. You must fight. Turn to 343 for rules on phaser combat, but *remember this reference* so that you can return afterwards.

Scavenger   SKILL 8

If you wish to avoid this fight, you may contact the ship and beam back aboard out of harm's way (turn to 141) although you will be condemning Dilane to certain death. If you win the fight, turn to 152.

197

You call all your section heads to the briefing room and explain to them the necessity of keeping up the crew's morale. You do not yet have enough information to guide the ship to your escape route and you must keep searching, but you are confident that you will eventually discover the whereabouts of a suitable black hole. Turn to 80.

198

Leaving orbit you do a long-range scan. Two stars ahead have planets which may sustain life orbiting them. One star is purple in colour – if you wish to head for this one turn to 44. The other is a double star which you may head towards by turning to 333.

199

Following their directions, you head towards the hills to visit the Rain Lord's castle. After some fifteen minutes' walk you see a large building in the distance and it takes you another fifteen minutes to reach it. Evidently a walk which takes you half an hour would take the aliens much longer at their sluggish pace. You reach the gate and can see an armed guard barring the way. Will you draw your phasers and shoot at the guard (turn to **61**) or continue up to the gate to talk to the guard (turn to **237**)?

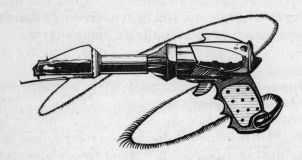

200

You set your phaser to *kill* and fire at the first creature. Your blast causes it to bellow loudly before it drops to the ground, dead. But its cry has alerted the other two and they charge towards you. Your second shot stops one in its tracks. If you have no other crew members with you here, turn to **243**. If you still have at least one other companion, turn to **279**.

201

Your crew send the plane off into space. It enters the planet's atmosphere and hurtles down to crash on to the surface. You wait, and some moments later a report comes through. It seems that, whatever it is, this killer has spread into the Engineering Section, as two men have dropped dead. One of these may be your Engineering Officer, as he was at work there. Throw two dice. If you roll a double 1 or double 6, your Engineering Officer has died. Turn to **172**.

202

After several hours of sub-light travel, you reach the Ganzigite starbase. It is a huge, doughnut-shaped structure, rotating slowly in space. You are instructed to hold the *Traveller* in orbit and beam down to meet the Imperial High Commander.

Your encounter with the Commander is enlightening. He realizes you are indeed lost in space and in the interests of his own security he wishes you to find your way back to your own universe. This you will only be able to do by returning through a space warp created by a black hole. The timing and location will be critical. He cannot provide any more useful information but is sure that other planets may be able to help you, suggesting that you explore this galaxy for the correct time and location coordinates.

For your part, you feed him with information about your own galaxy. He is disturbed by your ship's offensive weapons but agrees to release you if he may insert a subroutine into your target tracking program such that you will never be able to fire on Imperial Ganzig Confederation ships during the rest of your voyage. You agree, and from now on, you will not be able to fire phasers at these ships (make a note of this).

You beam back to your ship and plan your search for the time and location coordinates. Turn to **16**.

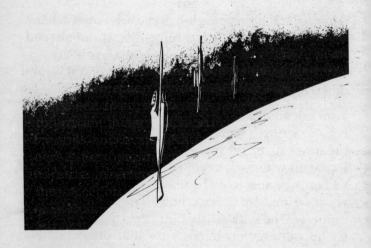

203

You leave orbit and probe with your scanners for likely destinations. Some 3·3 light years away is a large red planet which you can head towards. Turn to **126**.

204

Watching and listening on your monitor, you suddenly hear your officer shouting in an excited voice. It seems he has found dilibrium deposits in another asteroid, away from the central cluster! He jets across to investigate and commences mining with his micro-excavator. Throw one die. If you roll a 4, 5 or 6, he finds enough raw material to continue the journey, and may return to the ship with it (turn to **165**). If you roll a 1, 2 or 3, there is insufficient ore on that asteroid and he will still have to continue to the central cluster (turn to **47**).

205

You stand alone with I-Abail. Quickly, you pull out your phaser and train it on him. 'Stranger,' he says, 'you may put down your weapon. I am unarmed and will do you no harm.' Still, you do not trust him and, flicking your communicator open, you call the ship and give instructions for you to be beamed back aboard. Turn to **41**.

206

Roll one die. If you roll anything from 1 to 5, one of your companions (you choose) fires at the leader. If you roll a 6, you fire.

The blast hits the leader – and has no effect whatsoever! Perhaps their armour is blast-resistant or perhaps they are just invulnerable to phaser fire. Turning towards whoever fired the shot, the leader points his finger and an electric blue ray shoots from the tip right through his aggressor. If this was you, you are now dead and your adventure is over. If this was one of your companions, he is dead. After this incident you feel you have no choice but to climb into their vehicle. Turn to **317**.

207

Your nearest destination is a large grey planet some 2·3 light years ahead. You set course and enter warp speed, dropping out again a short distance from this planet. Turn to **253**.

Your officer tells your crew to defend themselves. The guards point their weapons and fire as your crew duck and dodge. They take on one guard each. Choose which crew member will attack which guard and join battle. For hand-to-hand combat rules, turn to **342** – but *remember this reference* so that you can return afterwards.

	SKILL	STAMINA
First guard	6	7
Second guard	7	6

You, meanwhile, are torn in your allegiance. Part of you wishes to help your crew, and part of you wants to aid the guards. After each set of attack rounds for the two skirmishes going on, roll one die. If you roll a 1, you will attack one of your own crew members (you choose) for 1 point of STAMINA damage. If you roll a 6, you will attack one of the guards for 1 point of STAMINA damage. If you roll anything from 2 to 5, you are too confused to attack either.

If your crew defeat both guards, turn to **48**. If either of your crew members is reduced to a STAMINA score of 3 or less, your most senior officer orders the fight to stop – turn to **234**.

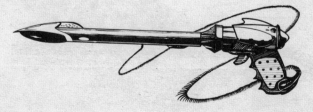

209

You materialize on the planet surface and look around. You are in a wide street of some kind, which is completely deserted. Buildings, of sorts, line the street and behind you a large building stands at the end of the road. The buildings are strange structures. They are a multitude of shapes and sizes and all look incomplete. You may either:

Continue down the road looking for signs of life	Turn to **125**
Approach the large building behind you	Turn to **73**
Try one of the smaller buildings	Turn to **231**

210

Your MO returns and complains of feeling unwell. Roll two dice and compare the total with your LUCK score. If the total is *equal to or higher than* your LUCK, turn to **107**. If it is *lower* than your LUCK, turn to **219**.

211

You set course and arrive at the black hole, dropping out of warp speed some distance from it. Carefully planning your angle of entry and velocity, you head into the dark void. You feel the ship being taken by the immense gravitational force and order all crew to strap themselves in. Suddenly the ship lurches forwards and begins to speed up. The G-force is so strong that you, along with the rest of the crew, pass out. Turn to **339**.

212

You enter the bar. It is a dingy, smoky room and a variety of aliens of all shapes and sizes are sitting drinking colourful drinks. They all look at you inquisitively as you enter – you must look extremely unusual to them – and one of them grunts at you. You decide not to waste time here. You may find another Service Robot and ask to see someone in authority (turn to 74) or make arrangements to have your ship serviced (turn to 106).

213

After running several tests, your MO discovers a strange micro-organism in the patient's bloodstream. Trying various antibiotics, she finally comes up with an effective one and administers what she hopes will be the cure. Some time later, the patient wakes up with a terrible headache, but cured of his madness. You must now continue on your journey. Turn to 336.

214

The path twists and you arrive at another fork. Do you wish to take the left-hand fork (turn to 318) or the right-hand fork (turn to 305)?

215

Following the guard, you turn down another corridor which leads to a large, open room. Various armoured guards seem to be directing civilians through a large open doorway at one end of the room from which a dull red glow is coming. You are directed to the end of the line. Do you have your Science Officer with you? If so, turn to **33**. If you have already tried to contact the ship, turn to **238**. Otherwise, turn to **309**.

216

You call all your section heads to the briefing room and announce that you believe you have the space and time coordinates for a likely black hole. If your velocity and timing are right, you ought to be able to pass through this black hole, which may be the Seltsian Void, and emerge in Earth's universe. You return to the bridge and prepare for the journey, setting off towards your black hole. Subtract its time coordinates from its location coordinates and turn to the number that this gives.

217

Dodging several small asteroids, your officer arrives at his destination. Drawing a micro-excavator from his belt he sets to work on mining the crystal ore. You are watching his progress on your viewer. After several minutes he checks the readings on his scanner and reports that he has only one kilo of raw material, not enough to fuel your ship. He will have to try one of the other asteroids. Which will he go for?

The first asteroid	Turn to **30**
The second asteroid	Turn to **96**
The fourth asteroid	Turn to **295**

218

She is rather reluctant but eventually agrees to show you a little more of the planet. You leave the building through a heavy doorway and the scene outside is chaotic. Buildings are in ruins; no one walks in the streets; apart from two or three small skycars, the whole planet appears to have been devastated.

'The entire population,' explains Dilane, 'lives in protection domes. Our planet is dying, being ripped apart from the gravitational variations caused by our two suns. We are at the moment constructing ships to take our people to another planet before the world is destroyed.'

Would you like to explore the city further (turn to 265)? If not, you may either ask whether they may be able to help with your return to Earth (turn to 169) or ask if there is anything you may be able to do to help them (turn to 319).

219

The illness develops and your MO begins to sweat profusely with a fever. Will you take your Medical Officer back to the ship for help (turn to 146) or continue your investigations on the planet (turn to 249)?

220

Turning the corner, you continue for several metres. A noise behind you startles you and you stop. With a sudden chill of panic, you realize what the noise is – it is the multiple hammer sound of a pre-laser weapon. Someone, or something, is firing a machine gun at you! You drop to the ground and scream at your companions to do likewise. As you all lie there with bullets flying over your heads, the other two look at you, puzzled. 'Captain, why are we lying in the road?' says one of them, standing up. To your amazement he stands in the hail of bullets, completely unharmed! Gradually the sound fades and the others help you to your feet, looking at you in a most peculiar way.

A little further down the road you come across a large building. Will you enter this building (turn to 55) or continue down the road turn to (325)?

The Dar-Villian Commander uses a device on his wrist to contact his headquarters. Over several minutes, he speaks to various members of his personnel. Finally one of them evidently has a good idea; the Commander turns to you. 'Since your two bodies were combined by a transmatter beam,' he reasons, 'it seems logical that you should be separated in the same way.' His idea is to focus two transmatter beams on your coordinates (one being the ship's and the other from his own headquarters) at exactly the same time. This should separate your two selves, hopefully into their two original identities. If you wish to try this, turn to 162. If it sounds too risky, you may ask your Science Officer for his suggestions (turn to 35) or consult the ship's computer (turn to 299).

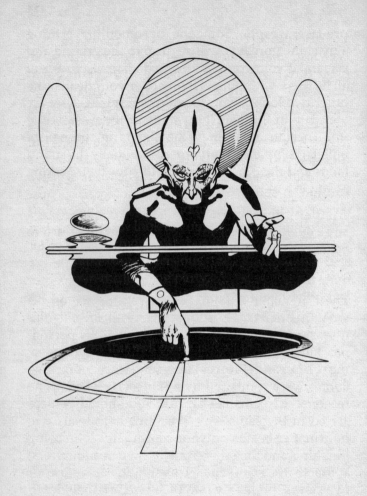

222

As you appear in his office, I-Abail comes forward to greet you. From his surroundings, you deduce that his society is indeed sophisticated, with a technology far more advanced than your own. The surface of his desk floats in the air and he sits behind it, apparently on thin air. He invites you to sit, but there are no chairs. Cautiously you sit as he has done and some unseen force takes your weight. Around the walls are moving holograms, positioned as an Earth executive may have works of art hanging in his office. To the side of his desk is a screen which he talks into. Moments later, another alien arrives with a tray of what you assume are refreshments. I-Abail introduces this newcomer and offers you food and drink. Will you accept his offer (turn to 98) or will you thank him, but politely decline (turn to 144)?

223

Roll two dice for your Medical Officer. If the roll is *equal to or lower than* her SKILL score, turn to 129. If the roll *exceeds* her SKILL, turn to 46.

224

Your Science Officer believes it is not possible for these creatures to be so powerful without some sort of energy pack. As it does not look as though such a device is hidden in their armour, it must be under their helmets. You may be able to disable them by removing their helmets. If you wish to try removing a helmet, turn to 49. Otherwise turn to 309.

225

You realize you must have chosen the wrong coordinates and contact the ship. You have yourselves beamed back aboard and then beamed down to the correct coordinates, 223.473.83. Turn to **57**.

226

Sensors scan the asteroid cluster. In the centre of the cluster is an asteroid containing some dilibrium, but it is impossible at this range to ascertain exactly which asteroid has the mineral. You may investigate by sending out one of your officers with a jet pack, but the going will be dangerous. The centre of the cluster is a mass of whirling asteroids, each one big enough to kill a man. Will you risk sending one of your crew (turn to **327**) or will you decide against taking the risk and head onwards (turn to **69**)?

227

Throw two dice. If the number thrown is *higher* than your Science Officer's SKILL, turn to **282**. If the number is *equal to or less than* your SO's SKILL, turn to **83**.

228

Straining in his seat, your navigation officer checks your position. You have changed your course, but unfortunately so has the meteor storm, and you are still heading into it. Activate your shields and turn to **283**.

229

Luff now asks you to keep your part of the bargain and transport him and his technical staff to the ship to investigate your weapons and defence systems. Will you honour your agreement with him? If so, turn to **191**. If you refuse, turn to **298**.

230

If you have selected your Science Officer to accompany you, turn to **56**. If you have selected your Engineering Officer, turn to **277**. If you have selected both, you may turn to either reference, but if you have chosen neither, turn to **151**.

231

You arrive at an odd-shaped building with rounded walls. Several strange and apparently meaningless sticks protrude from the front walls. The door is open and you cautiously walk inside. Slumped over a table is a bulky figure, apparently asleep. Your entrance disturbs the creature and it raises its head, sees you, and springs to its . . . foot! Rather than legs, it has a single stump, something like a tree-trunk. It bellows loudly and your translator does not translate. Will you:

Hold your hands up to show you
    mean no harm?   Turn to 42
Draw your phasers and shoot?   Turn to 334

You step into space and, to your surprise, your foot touches something solid which bears your weight. Moving forwards, you hear an electrical buzz and a flash of light blinds you momentarily. When you open your eyes you find yourself back in the portal lab, with I-Abail and his technicians watching you. They rush forward to congratulate you. Their experiment has been successful! As I-Abail takes you from the lab back to his office, he explains that they were able to monitor your activities with their instruments and that the experiment has answered several of the unknowns that they had come across in their investigations.

However, although their portal may transport your crew back to your own universe, they would be stranded without the ship. The ship would need a much bigger portal but their investigations indicate that such a portal will occur naturally at a certain time in the vicinity of a black hole in Sector 159. I-Abail shows you, on a star chart, where Sector 159 is; you ask about other planets in the galaxy. He is unable to give details, but suggests you head for Malini, a mining planet several light years away. You contact the ship and beam back aboard. Turn to 41.

As you travel towards your destination, your language lab reports some interesting findings from the newspaper you gave them. You have just come from the planet Prax, a fairly advanced civilization. Some years before the paper was published, a great debate occurred and two groups emerged with two schools of thought. The Progressives were modern thinkers, set on material progress, computerization and a more scientific view of the future. The Regressives, on the other hand, disliked the inhuman element of the Progressives' world and preferred a return to basics, where people did not rely on machines. A period of cold war ensued, until the Regressives discovered that the Progressives had developed a powerful hallucinatory drug. The Progressives had intended to use the drug on the Regressives, but when the plot was discovered, they agreed to send all stocks of the drug into space out of the way. Something went wrong, however, and the rocket exploded in the planet's upper atmosphere, subjecting the entire planet to severe hallucinations. On the day the paper was published, its effects were just beginning to be noticed.

You may continue your course, heading either to the purple star (turn to 44) or the small star cluster (turn to 79).

234
Your officer tells your crew not to resist arrest. The guards take your weapons and march you off. As you are led away, you experience an uncontrollable desire to scream, and you utter a strange sentence in Dar-Villian. Commander Domm answers you, saying you will be called for later. Turn to **95**.

235
Another blast narrowly misses the ship and you decide to retaliate. For ship-to-ship combat rules, turn to **341** but *remember this reference* so that you can return afterwards.

Alien ship   WEAPONS STRENGTH 8   SHIELDS 7

If you destroy your opponent, turn to **133**.

236

You search for suitable plants, using a nutritional analyser to tell you which will be edible. Not far from where you landed, you find a small cluster of suitable plants with succulent leaves, large fruits and tuberous roots. You begin to cut down the plants and make them into a pile which may be beamed up to the ship.

Suddenly, you feel something restraining your leg and look down to see a vine wrapped round your calf. Its grip tightens. As you wrestle with the vine, the leaves of another plant bend over your head and clamp themselves on to your body. You struggle, but it seems that the plants are alive and are attempting to defend themselves against you! Will you draw your phaser and attempt to cut yourself free (turn to 45) or will you decide not to risk harming the plants further and try to untangle yourself (turn to 87)?

237

The guard sees you and flurries into action. Raising its head in the air, it lets out a shrill whistle. Seconds later you look up to see that you are surrounded by alien guards, all with weapons pointed at you. You decide it best to surrender to them. Turn to 315.

238

Remembering what happened last time you tried your communicator, you try contacting the ship. Again you are unable to get through and hear nothing but static, but your communicator again has its strange effect on the aliens. You are looking at a room full of statues; the aliens are transfixed. This is an opportune time to leave the room. Turn to **160**.

239

The guards escort you to another room where you are instructed to change into tight-fitting uniforms. You are given sturdy helmets to wear and a choice of strange weapons. The guards will tell you nothing of your event, but lead you from the room down a tunnel.

Your heart sinks as you emerge from the tunnel. You stand in a vast arena and the alien cheers are deafening. In the centre of the arena is a large, dark Manslayer Robot, heavily armed. The door behind you slams shut and the Manslayer advances. Evidently you must defeat this robot before it kills you! In this fight, the robot is powerful enough to fight all of you every attack round (i.e. however many there are of you, it will fight each of you in separate combat). However, your weapons are particularly effective and you need make no SKILL deductions for crew members unskilled in fighting. For hand-to-hand combat rules turn to **342** but *remember this reference* so that you can return afterwards.

Manslayer Robot SKILL 10 STAMINA 4

As soon as any of your party inflicts a hit on the robot, turn to **183**.

240

After two rounds of combat, the Security Guards have reached you. Throw one die. If the number is 5 or 6, the guards manage to hold him and the fight ends. If the fight has not ended (1, 2, 3 or 4), you must have another bout of combat – roll again to see whether the guards are able to capture him this time or whether yet another round is necessary. Continue until they are able to hold him. Then you may either call for a medical team (turn to **128**) or get a report on the planet (turn to **302**).

241

Your phaser stuns the little creature, who drops to the ground. The spider-like alien nursing his leg gasps in horror. 'No, no! That is very good. You should not have done that!' Your group closes ranks as several aliens emerge from nearby doorways. Although all appear to be of different species, it is clear that they all regard you with hostility and they are advancing. Your crew shuffles nervously.

A groan comes from the small beast lying on the ground. It raises its head and slowly rises to its feet. The effect of your phaser has worn off. The advancing aliens stop, and mutter at each other. Seeing their neighbour is safe, they return to their buildings. You give a sigh of relief and turn to the spider creature on the floor. Turn to **19**.

242

Starting up the ship's engines, you leave the spaceport and head off into deep space. Turn to 324.

243

You are unable to aim in time. The great beast is upon you, its stumpy leg poised to crush you. You try to dive out of the way, but the undergrowth is too thick and you cry out in pain as it deals a deadly blow. Your adventure is over.

244

You approach the castle gates. Using your phasers, you melt the lock and open the large doors. Inside you proceed with caution, keeping hidden in the shadows as you make your way towards the central keep. From the activity you see inside, it seems most likely that you will find the Rain Lord in this central building. However, there are three guards on the door, all armed with the missile sticks your original hosts were carrying. You may either approach these guards and demand to be taken to the Rain Lord (turn to 274) or open fire with your phasers (turn to 131).

245

The eagle flies from its perch and swoops down on the intruder. In abject terror, the alien swipes at the bird as it attacks. You watch the battle. For personal combat rules, turn to **342** – but *remember this reference* so that you can return afterwards.

	SKILL	STAMINA
Eagle	6	5
Ganzigite	10	10

Deduct 2 points from the Ganzigite's SKILL for its fear of the eagle. As soon as the alien inflicts any damage on the eagle, turn to **188**.

246

You step off the path. To your horror, you fall through space. You pass the pathways and fall through blackness. You are stranded in limbo between two universes. The space portal experiment has not worked and you will never see the *Traveller* again!

247

You are powerless to prevent the Macommonians carrying out their plan. After an hour, a duplicate of yourself stands before you and speaks in your voice! Using your own communicator, the impostor orders the entire crew to beam down. They transport to the surface as ordered and, as they land, they are taken prisoner while the Macommonians beam up to take over the ship.

You are doomed to spend the next year in a detention cell before being destroyed with the planet; you will never see Earth again.

248

You approach a small blue-green planet and take up an orbital position. You scan the planet for signs of life. It appears to be lifeless but the scanners are giving some strange readings which you cannot understand. You try an all-frequency radio message but receive no answer.

Suddenly, the scanners pick up a signal – probably a ship of some kind – travelling towards you extremely fast in orbit from the other side of the planet! You switch to visual and can see a missile-shaped object hurtling towards you. You hit the red alert button and activate shields, waiting to see what happens. From nowhere a blast hits the ship. Roll two dice. If the roll is *equal to or lower than* your SHIELDS score, deduct 1 point from SHIELDS. If the roll *exceeds* your SHIELDS score, deduct 2 points from SHIELDS. If you roll a double 6, deduct 5 points from SHIELDS.

Will you try to contact the object as it closes (turn to 58) or will you go immediately to battle stations (turn to 235)?

249

While you question the alien Elder, your Medical Officer's health deteriorates rapidly. You are called back to look at the MO but arrive just too late to prevent her death. You must decide what to do next. Turn to 304.

250

The next solar system likely to contain life-bearing planets is some 2·2 light years away. You enter warp drive and head onwards, leaving hyperspace as you approach this solar system some time later. Turn to **34**.

251

The Dar-Villian Commander shouts angrily. It appears that he believes this is some sort of trick. He orders his guards to arrest you and your crew and to take you to a detention centre. The crew look to you, wondering whether or not to resist this arrest, but you are in no position to make any decisions. Choose your most senior officer in the landing party and roll two dice. If the number rolled is *higher* than that officer's SKILL score, turn to **234**. If it is *equal to or less than* his SKILL score, turn to **208**. Remember to deduct 3 points from his SKILL on this roll as he is making a leadership decision and he is not skilled in leadership.

252

Energizing his jet pack, your officer manages to leap clear of the asteroid as the two great boulders collide. Breathing a sigh of relief, he turns back towards the ship, arriving safely with several kilos of dilibrium ore. Turn to **165**.

253

Sensors indicate that you are travelling past a large spaceport some distance to starboard. If your ship is

damaged you may wish to dock for repairs (turn to
52). Otherwise you may continue onwards (turn to
109).

254

The ship lurches hard to port. The crew are unpre-
pared for this violent shift and fall to the floor
around you. Throw one die for each crew member
listed on your *Adventure Sheet*. A throw of 1 to 5
means they escape injury with only minor bruises.
A throw of 6 means that they are badly injured as
they collide with a wall.

Each badly injured crew member is rushed to the
Medical Section. They will be healed if the Medical
Officer can roll a number on two dice *equal to or less
than* her SKILL score. If not, the injury is serious and
that crew member will play no further part in the
adventure. Repeat this roll for each crew member
who has been badly injured.

Now roll two dice and compare the result with your
LUCK score. If the number rolled is *equal to or lower
than* your LUCK score, turn to **167**. If it is *higher*, turn
to **228**.

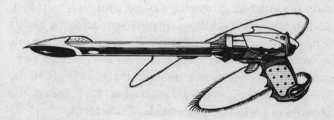

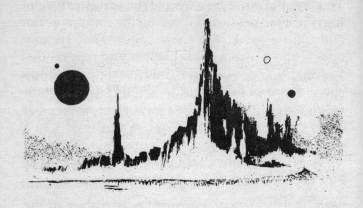

255

Your Science Officer suggests that these mysterious deaths are most likely caused by some sort of microorganism picked up from the planet. He will do some tests on the bodies and will ask the Medical Officer to spray the area with antibiotic. You agree.

You wait to hear the results. Meanwhile, another report reaches you. The deaths have spread from the engineering section to the medical section. You may lose your Engineering and Medical Officers. Throw two dice once for each. If you roll any double or 7 for your Engineering Officer, he has been lost, as the mysterious killer has now spread through the Engineering Section. If you roll a double 1 or double 6, your Medical Officer dies. You decide you must prevent the spread of this killer by sealing off all the infected areas, even though this may mean the deaths of crew trapped inside. Turn to **18**.

256

You and the other members of the crew are regaining consciousness. Again you hit the communicator and call for systems damage reports. All systems appear to be intact, until Engineering reports that the warp drive engines are dead. You are floating in space! But your drive reactors should be operational in twenty to thirty minutes.

Your navigation officer is bewildered. He cannot identify your whereabouts and the computer reports you are in uncharted space. Your Science Officer has run an event analysis and you appear to have gone through the black hole, through a dimension warp, and you are now in what seems to be a parallel universe.

After some delay you regain warp drive. Long-range scan indicates three solar systems ahead, of which two may have intelligent life. Will you:

Press on towards the life-
bearing system ahead?   Turn to **86**
Turn to port towards the other
life-bearing system?   Turn to **273**
Turn to starboard towards the
barren system?   Turn to **142**

257

You set off again towards the large grey planet. But have your landing party contracted the infection? Throw one die for each crew member (including yourself) who entered the spaceport. A roll of 5 or 6 means that that person is infected. Your Medical Officer tries to find a cure; she will succeed if you roll a number *less than* her SKILL score on two dice. Otherwise, the infected crew members will slowly die. You must deduct 2 SKILL and 4 STAMINA points from each, and you must cross them off your *Adventure Sheet* when they eventually die after leaving the next planet. Turn to **109**.

258

You approach the large red planet at sub-light speed and set an orbiting course. Scanning the surface, you find no trace of intelligent life, but signs of civilization – and a fairly advanced one at that – are apparent. As you observe the planet through your macro-telescope, you see that the surface is covered in a network of roadways and canals, focused every so often at what must be a population centre of some sort. You try various radio frequencies but there is no response. Will you beam down on to the planet's surface (turn to **300**) or ignore this planet and continue onwards (turn to **163**)?

259

They take you through several buildings and then into a room where an old, wrinkled man sits at a desk. You greet him and explain your problem once more. The old man seems to have trouble understanding you and several times you have to repeat sections of your story. Suddenly, he seems to get very annoyed at you and commands you to leave his planet. Will you leave as he wishes (turn to **120**) or press him for information (turn to **54**)?

260

You settle the ship into orbit round the blue planet and check your scanners. It appears that the entire surface is covered in water, although there do seem to be life-forms within the water. You may either beam down, taking two crew members from your *Adventure Sheet* with you (turn to **288**) or leave orbit and head for the green planet (turn to **136**).

The planet appears to have no life on it, but scanners detect some sort of activity, perhaps the regular workings of a machine. You decide to investigate and send out a party in a recon plane to see what is happening. They pilot the plane to the area of the signal and land on the planet. It is rocky and barren but not far from where they have landed they find a scout ship of a type they have never come across before, crashed into the surface. Will you tell them to investigate it further (turn to **176**) or return to your ship (turn to **66**)?

You are now committed to leaving behind a certain number of crew members in exchange for docking and repair facilities at the starport. To determine who they will require you to assign to them, run down the following list throwing one die for each person. Each one that you roll a 6 for will have to remain at the starport when you leave and will play no further part in your adventure:

Science Officer	Ship's Hairdresser
Catering Officer	Engineering Officer
Administration Assistant	Electronics Expert
Entertainments Officer	Security Officer
Cleaner	Navigation Officer
Medical Officer	Ship's Cat

If you roll no sixes, you may assume that they ask for two general duty staff. If the price is more than three crew members, you may refuse to deal and leave the spaceport (turn to **324**). Otherwise, you agree to the deal and dock. Turn to **157**.

263

You wait until the vehicle approaches. It stops in front of you and three strange-looking aliens dressed in armoured uniforms spring out towards you. They are man-sized but somewhat insect-like, with spindly limbs and large eyes. They bark at you and your translator interprets: 'Out after curfew. This is illegal. You are strange and ugly. Where do you come from?' You try to relate your story. Turn to **140**.

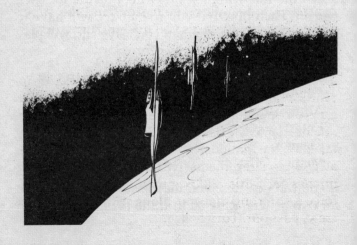

264

You land on a precipitous cliff overlooking a ravine. A terrible wind sweeps the land, which seems to be rocky and barren. As you cannot see much of interest from where you stand, you decide to descend the ravine, if only to shelter from the wind. Turn to **182**.

265

Dilane advises you against it, as the streets are dangerous and Scavengers are about. Scavengers are petty criminals living a life of looting and violence in the remains of the city. If you take her advice, turn to **218** and choose again. If you are determined to go on, turn to **196**.

266

The supervisor listens to your story and tries to contact K'tait to confirm it. Eventually he makes contact. K'tait confirms your story and the supervisor, apologizing, takes you to him. Turn to **134**.

267

You set course and arrive at the black hole, dropping out of warp speed some distance from it. Carefully planning your angle of entry and velocity, you head into the dark void. You feel the ship being taken by the immense gravitational force and order all crew to strap themselves in. Suddenly the ship lurches forwards and begins to speed up. The G-force is so strong that you, along with the rest of the crew, pass out. Turn to **339**.

268

Roll two dice and compare the score with your Engineering Officer's SKILL. If the roll *equals or exceeds* this, turn to **139**. If the roll is *less than* his SKILL, turn to **70**.

269

Leaving orbit, you scan space ahead of you. There is a planet ahead, some 3·6 light years away, which may support life. You enter warp speed and head towards it. The electronics lab reports that the helmet you brought back was indeed an advanced piece of work. With a few adjustments, they will be able to prepare it so that, when you wear it, you may increase your SKILL by 1 point. This will undoubtedly be useful. Turn to **34**.

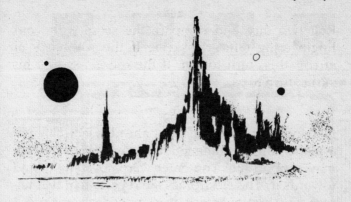

270

You plot a course and leave orbit, entering warp speed towards the purple planet. A message comes up through the intercom of a disturbance in the ship's canteen and you are asked to attend straight away. Turn to **314**.

271

As you reel from the blow, you fall backwards into the arms of I-Abail, who holds you. Forcing you towards the portal, he shoves you forwards through the frame. Turn to **53**.

272

The extreme temperature on the planet prevents your scanner from functioning properly. There is no way of telling whether or not life exists here. Will you explore further on foot (turn to **159**) or abandon this inhospitable planet and return to the ship (turn to **31**)?

273

You travel ahead at sub-warp speed to allow your sensors to scan for information. They pick up a small object several thousand kilometres ahead and travelling towards you. You continue cautiously.

At five kilometres it stops – and you do likewise. Sensors report a Class D starcruiser and you prepare yourself with shields up. A message comes in and you transfer it to the screen.

A reptilian face appears in a uniform of authority. As your translator tunes in, the alien's message becomes clear:

> 'I am Commander M'k Tel of the Imperial Ganzig Confederation. You are a non-registered ship trespassing within Imperial territory. Identify yourself and state your purpose.'

What will your reply be?

Identify yourself as he wishes	Turn to **281**
Run an InfoScan on the Imperial Ganzig Confederation	Turn to **51**
Open fire	Turn to **135**

274

They spring to attention as you approach, levelling their sticks at you. One of your party reacts in haste, going for his phaser, and a missile shoots from the end of one of the guards' sticks, hitting him square in the chest. Throw a die for each crew member; the one with the highest score has been hit and is seriously wounded. If you have your Medical Officer with you, throw two dice. If you roll *less* than your MO's SKILL, your over-anxious crew member will not die, but may take no further part in the action until he is returned to the ship. If you do not have your MO or if the number rolled *equals or exceeds* your MO's SKILL, you cannot save this crew member and he drops down dead.

The guards keep you covered and usher you into the keep. Turn to **91**.

275

Your Science Officer suggests that you have been beamed down to the exact coordinates where one of the Dar-Villian officers was standing and that your bodies have merged. He and the Commander agree that a solution must be found to separate the two individuals once more. Turn to **124**.

276

You call the ship and instruct the Transmatter Unit to beam one aboard and beam down a replacement (choose from your available officers/security staff). Your companion protests loudly that he has just saved your life, but moments later, he disappears and his replacement appears. You step over the body and continue. Turn to **220**.

277

You materialize on the planet surface. Your Engineering Officer checks his portable scanner and is extremely interested in a large rock behind you. He has found an energy source of some kind within the rock and chips away some of the black surface. Beneath the surface covering is a fluorescent green metal and he cuts out a large chunk to take back to the ship with him. If you have your Science Officer with you, turn to 56. If not, turn to 151.

278

The ship begins to shudder but your scanners indicate you are not far from your destination, the small blue-green planet ahead. To the great relief of your crew you order engineering to cut warp engines and slow down to sub-light speed in order to approach the planet. Turn to 248; this planet is your last hope – will it provide dilibrium ore for you?

279

The last remaining beast is almost on top of you. You dive out of the way, but as you do so, you hear another great bellow. Picking yourself up, you find that your companion has killed the creature less than a metre from you! You contact the ship and have yourselves beamed back aboard, along with your prey. Turn to 311.

280

He takes you to his Astronautical Headquarters and has words with the Director of Operations, who disappears into another room and returns with a printout. So far as his department can ascertain, the black hole you require is in Sector 083, but he cannot be sure of the correct timing. You thank him for the information and return to the ship to continue your journey. Turn to **320**.

281

You explain to the Commander who you are and how you came to be in his territory. He is suspicious. He claims you as a prisoner and says he will escort you back to his starbase where your story can be considered by his superiors. He instructs you to prepare your Transmatter Unit to receive his First Officer, who will accompany you. Will you:

Comply with his wishes?	Turn to **168**
Switch off the screen and activate phasers?	Turn to **135**

282

Your Science Officer tries for some time to follow the computer's weather control program, but the language is sophisticated and he is unable to make sense of it. After some hours he is forced to admit that he is unlikely to get anywhere with it. Unable to help, your party must return to the ship to continue your journey. Turn to **203**.

283

Unavoidably heading into the meteor storm, you sit tight and hope it will pass quickly. As you enter, the

Traveller rocks as the shields take blows from the pounding meteors.

Throw one die ten times. Each time you throw a 6, a meteor penetrates your shields and damages the ship. For each penetration, throw two dice. A roll *equal to or less than* your SHIELDS score will do minor damage (deduct 1 point from your SHIELDS score). A roll *greater* than your SHIELDS score will do 2 points worth of damage to your shields. If you roll a double 6, the meteor hits a vital part of the ship's hull; deduct 5 points from your SHIELDS score.

If, after ten throws, your ship has not been destroyed, you sail through the meteor storm and can proceed to the small star cluster you were originally heading for. Turn to **60**.

284

You give the instruction to evacuate all air from the affected area, and all crew within the area are instructed to wear EVA (Extra Vehicular Activity) suits, as they will be in a vacuum. The air is pumped out into space and, half an hour later, fresh air is introduced. Your Science Officer checks this new air and it is found to be poison-free. Turn to **11**.

285

Scanning the planet, you are relieved to find an area of dilibrium ore deposits. You may choose two other crew members from the *Adventure Sheet* to accompany you and you beam down to the mineral-rich area.

The planet is barren and rocky. A howling wind blasts across the planet's surface. Using a portable scanner, you locate a deposit of crystal ore and instruct one of your crew members to collect several kilos with his micro-excavator. Before returning to the ship you decide to investigate the planet a little more, starting with a ravine several hundred metres ahead. Turn to **182**.

286

On your instruction, the crew of the *Traveller* begin beaming down, grateful for the chance of a rest. You meet them in one of the large domes. With the ship set to automatic pilot, the entire crew are eventually with you. Dilane leaves the room to arrange transport but, after she leaves, you find the exit door is locked! Moments later one of your crew points to a small duct in the ceiling, where a yellow vapour is seeping into the room. You feel drowsy and your crew are beginning to pass out around you. You fall to the ground unconscious.

You awake in another similar dome. Around you, the crew are also beginning to stir. Through a hidden speaker, Dilane's voice comes over: 'I am sorry, Captain, that this was necessary. We Macommonians have less than a year left before our planet is destroyed. We must have your ship if we are to survive as a race. Thank you for your sacrifice.'

You and your crew are trapped in a Macommonian detention cell. In a year's time you will be destroyed with the planet; you will never see the *Traveller* again.

287

You wait for perhaps an hour but K'tait does not return. The door opens and a hover-robot enters the room. It stops abruptly as it senses you and various whirrings indicate it is contacting its central processor. It speaks to you, telling you to follow it. If you consent to follow it, turn to **195**. If you insist on waiting for K'tait, turn to **29**.

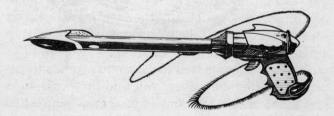

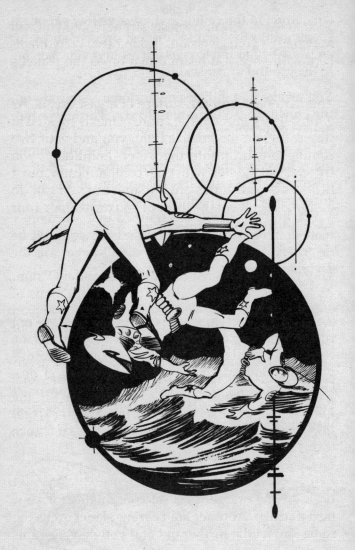

288

Your Science Officer protests strongly, but you will not change your decision. Taking two crew members with you, you beam down on to the planet's surface.

You materialize on the surface of a vast ocean. As your sensors warned, the entire planet is covered in water. As you materialize fully, you and your two companions drop into the water. Frantically, you try to signal the ship with your communicator, but it is no use. Your lungs are bursting but you can do nothing to prevent the three of you drowning. Your adventure is over . . .

289

Your Science Officer speaks to Commander Domm. As he does so, you realize the full implications of what has happened. You also feel turmoil going on inside you. You question what has happened but your voice is that of a Dar-Villian and a powerful aggressive feeling, part hatred, part panic overcomes you. Roll two dice and compare the total with your Science Officer's SKILL score. If the number rolled is *equal to or less than* that SKILL score, turn to 275. If the roll *exceeds* your SO's SKILL, turn to 251.

290

Back on the bridge, you set coordinates for your next journey. Another life-bearing planet orbits the same sun a little further out and you may visit this next (turn to **258**), or you may head further onwards towards a purple sun some light years away (turn to **44**).

291

The alien is quite a talkative creature and tells you that you are on the planet Cliba. On the surface of the planet there are many villages of similar creatures. Their stage of cultural development seems to approximate that of the Middle Ages on Earth. They are an agricultural race; the weather on the planet used to be excellent but bad weather has ruined their crops for several seasons. The weather is controlled by someone they refer to as the 'Rain Lord', who lives in a fortified castle, two hours' journey from their village. The Rain Lord is, they believe, punishing them with this bad weather. As the crops have been failing, the village has been hit by famine and disease. If you have your Medical Officer with you, you may offer to see what can be done for the sick (turn to **101**). You may ask them whether they have any knowledge of astronomy (turn to **155**), or you may offer to try to contact the Rain Lord (turn to **199**).

292

Turn to **233**.

293

The path continues ahead and a short distance on forks again. Will you take the left-hand fork (turn to **322**) or the right-hand fork (turn to **338**)?

294

You explain that you have no currency and ask if there is anything else they would accept. The only needs they have are food and personnel, and they are willing to let you dock if you will order one, or some, of your crew to remain permanently assigned to the spaceport. There is a general consensus amongst the crew that they would be willing to sacrifice themselves in the interests of saving the ship, but will you allow them to go? If so, turn to **262** to see who you will have to lose. Otherwise you can refuse their offer and leave (turn to **324**).

295

Landing on the asteroid, your officer draws his micro-excavator from his belt and sets to work, piling fragments of rock into his portasack. From the ship you watch his progress on the viewer. Suddenly a large asteroid comes into view heading straight for your officer! You hit your communicator and shout a quick warning – but are you too late? Throw one die. If you throw a 1 or 2, turn to **110**. If you throw a 3, 4, 5 or 6, turn to **252**.

296

You train your scanners on space, searching for your next destination. It appears that there are no life-supporting planets within range. You decide to try a hyperspace jump into another sector of space. Turn to **324**.

297

As you follow the armoured guard through a long tunnel, you seize your opportunity and spring. The creature is extremely strong but your numbers may give you the upper hand. For hand-to-hand combat rules, turn to **342**, but *remember this reference* so that you can return here afterwards. The guard will attack twice in a turn, so if three of you are attacking, you must decide (roll a die) to see which of you does not get attacked. If two of you are attacking, it will attack each of you and if you are attacking on your own, it will attack you twice (i.e. you get one roll for *Attack Strength*, it gets two; if both its rolls for *Attack Strength* are higher than yours, it does double damage).

Armoured guard   SKILL 11   STAMINA 14

If you defeat the guard, turn to **160**. If the battle is going badly, you may surrender, but only if you or one of your companions has been reduced to less than 4 STAMINA points. If you surrender, turn to **215**.

298

Three technical staff arrive, ready to beam aboard. They become extremely agitated as you try to avoid the issue. Suddenly, they pull out weapons and you will now have to fight them. For phaser combat rules, turn to **343**, but *remember this reference* so that you can return afterwards.

	SKILL
Luff	8
First technician	7
Second technician	6
Third technician	7

If you kill all the Terryals, you may beam back aboard ship. Turn to **120**.

299

The computer suggests you have your Engineering Officer rig up a genetic filter for the transmatter machine. Genetic filters are used in conjunction with transmatter devices in experimental genetics. When scientists wish to combine the features of two or more animals or plants to see what the resulting hybrid would be, they often use transmatter devices. If they wish to separate the resulting hybrid back again, they do so with a genetic filter which analyses the cellular make-up of an organism passing through the transmatter machine and separates the hybrid into its components. However, genetic filters are at an experimental stage only; often the results have been unexpected. If you wish to try this option, turn to **268**. If you don't want to take the risk, you may either turn to your Science Officer (turn to **35**) or ask the Dar-Villian's opinion (turn to **221**).

You choose a location within what ought to be one of the planet's main population centres. You select two crew members from the *Adventure Sheet* to accompany you to the planet's surface and the three of you beam down. When you re-materialize, you are in a deserted street. There is a ghostly silence about and something is not quite right. The buildings around you and the vehicles lying derelict by the side of the road appear to be from quite an advanced civilization, but dust is thick on everything, as if there has been no activity here for many years. Cautiously, you walk down the street. As you approach a junction at the end of the street, you hear a noise and stop. The others look at you quizzically, and listen . . . but they can hear nothing. You creep forwards towards the corner and jump back sharply as a shape appears.

'Visitors!' says a voice. The creature is roughly man-sized and wears a flowing white cape. 'We have not had visitors for many years.' You explain you are from another planet and the alien nods its hairy head. You ask whether it is possible to meet someone in a position of authority, and the creature considers for a moment.

Suddenly you hear a small click and a shrill buzzing noise, and the alien drops to the ground, scorched by a phaser blast from one of your party. You whirl round in disbelief. The attacker looks proudly at the dead alien and you order your other companion to hold him. Snatching his weapon, you demand to know why he fired at the alien. 'Why?' he gasps. 'If I hadn't fired he would have killed you! Did you not see the weapon in his hand aimed at you?' You certainly didn't see a weapon in the alien's hand, and neither did your other crew member. What will you do now?

Have your trigger-happy companion
  sent back to the ship?   Turn to 276
Beam the alien up to the ship
  to see whether anything can
  be done for him?   Turn to 112
Let your companion off with a
  caution and continue?   Turn to 220

301

You may contact the ship and beam back aboard quickly, ready to continue your journey. Turn to 320.

302

An analysis of all the data available on the deserted planet is run but no indication is given of the cause of the madness. The yellow powder seems to be an organic powder unlike anything known to your chemical analysts. You may, if you wish, make the enraged crew member take some of this powder, hoping that it will do some good (turn to 186). Otherwise you will have to call in a medical team (turn to 128).

303

Although you are powerless to prevent the duplicate being created, there is one scheme you can try to foil their plan. You concentrate hard. You will try to create a thought pattern in your mind which will give the ship's crew a clue as to what is happening. You fix two things in your mind: the truth – your doppelganger will not be able to lie if asked a direct question – and the planet Malthus-4.

After an hour or so the creation is ready and is led off to a communications room to transmit. Turn to **88**.

304

You may now either return to the ship to continue your voyage (turn to **203**) or offer to contact their Rain Lord to see if you can help them with their weather problem (turn to **199**).

305

You follow the path until it comes to an end in front of you. You may either step off the path into space (turn to **246**) or retrace your steps past the last junction to the previous one and turn to the right (turn to **113**).

306

The landing party are rushed off to the Medical Section for observation, but they appear to be fit and healthy. Meanwhile you receive another report. Three more crew members have mysteriously dropped dead, this time in the Engineering Section.

There is a chance that one of these will be your Engineering Officer. Throw two dice for each of these three victims. If you throw a double 6 or double 1, you have lost your Engineering Officer. Turn to **172**.

307

Remember this reference and turn to **343** for rules on phaser fire. You may try three shots at the creature before it runs back into its own building, and you must add 2 to your dice roll at each shot as the creature is a small, moving target. If you hit it, turn to **241**. If you miss, turn to **19**.

308

The Service Robot tells you the way to the Recreation Section. There is a games room and bar, along with a visi-room and sensorama. You may go on alone (turn to **212**) or you may return to the ship and invite the crew, as they could all do with a rest (turn to **65**).

309

The guards bundle you into line and you shuffle forwards with the others through the doorway into the red glow. You wait for an opportunity to escape. You cannot see what is happening through the door, as the air is fogged. You step through . . .

You have just stepped into an extermination chamber, a quick and painless method of keeping down the ever-expanding population on Culematter. Your journey has ended here.

310

Two guards appear to escort you to your seat. You are a little suspicious, as a sly smile spreads across K'Tait's face as you leave. You try to talk to the guards, but they are silent and you walk through a network of corridors. Turn to 239.

311

Back in the Transmatter Unit, the crew are taking your food off to the lab for analysis. You return to the bridge and prepare to leave orbit. The lab reports that your supplies are digestible and highly nutritious.

Scanners report the nearest planet some 3·7 light years from your present position. You set a course and enter warp speed. Turn to 34.

312

The path continues ahead and a short distance on forks again. Will you take the left-hand fork (turn to 20) or the right-hand fork (turn to 77)?

313

You spread yourselves out and wait, hoping the ship will realize you are in trouble and try a 'blind-beam' to rescue you. You continue to wait until it is difficult to breathe. A rock some distance to your left disappears, then another behind you, but the ship is unable to find your exact coordinates. You are now gasping, but you wait in vain. The ship is unable to find you and, as your air runs out, you collapse on the planet surface. Your journey has ended . . .

314

As you reach the canteen, excited crew members rush towards you. Although they are all talking at once, you get the general gist of what has happened. One of the crew seems to have gone mad. He has been throwing trays of food around the canteen and fighting with the other staff. You open the door and find him being held in a corner by three of the security crew, not an easy task. You recognize the trouble-maker and guess what has probably happened. He is the member of the landing party who took a drink on the barren planet you have just left. He is now a raging madman, straining against his captors, a heavy sweat on his red face and neck. Seeing you, he calms down. Will you:

Have him released and try to talk to him?	Turn to **102**
Call for a sedative drug from the Medical Section?	Turn to **128**
Ask for a report on the planet and the samples you brought back?	Turn to **302**

315

You are escorted into the castle towards a central keep, apparently the nerve centre of the castle. You explain that you wish to meet the Rain Lord. One of your guards goes off to the keep and comes back some moments later. Another group of guards comes over to take you inside the keep. Turn to **91**.

316

You leave orbit and increase speed. Will you head for a large grey planet (turn to 253) or search for an alternative destination (turn to 92)?

317

As you enter the vehicle it rocks from side to side. Your captors climb in and start the hover-engine, swinging the car round the way it came. You travel for half an hour or so and finally stop outside a large round building. Other similar cars have stopped there as well and numerous aliens are being led into the building. You are taken inside and put into a room which is evidently a cell of some kind, along with four aliens. They seem resigned to the fact that they are about to be exterminated as part of a population control programme. You cannot understand why they are so unemotional about their impending death.

One of the uniformed creatures calls for your party. You will have to act quickly. Will you try to fight your way out (turn to 297), try to contact the ship (turn to 67) or try to arrange to see someone in authority (turn to 121)?

318

The path twists and turns in space and you follow it to its end. There is no way forwards except by stepping off the path into space. If you wish to do this, turn to 232. If you wish to return to the previous fork and turn to the right, turn to 305.

319

'All we need,' says Dilane, 'are ships, and engineers to build more ships.'

You will not give her your ship, but you may give her your Engineering Officer if you wish. She promises that, if you do, she will give you useful information about returning to Earth. Will you assign your Engineering Officer to her (turn to **17**) or will you demur, saying you cannot leave your officers on alien planets (turn to **116**)?

320

You now have two choices: you may head towards a large, wheel-shaped structure hanging in space (turn to **137**) or you may enter hyperspace and jump towards a small black planet (turn to **331**).

321

Long-range scanners indicate another planet ahead, orbiting the same sun but some distance further out. You may continue to investigate this planet (turn to 258) or you may plot a course to avoid it (turn to 44).

322

The path bends round to the right and a short distance ahead forks again. Will you take the left-hand fork (turn to 113) or the right-hand fork (turn to 214)?

323

You have words with your Engineering and Science Officers. They agree it may be possible to divert power from either the phaser bank or the shields to

fuel the warp engines. You may choose either of
these sources and instruct the engineering crew to
begin work on the hook-up. However, you will be
vulnerable in battle until you find dilibrium ore or
crystal, and you must deduct 3 points from either
your WEAPONS STRENGTH or your SHIELDS score.
You may now continue on your journey. Turn to
248.

324

Your crew are becoming anxious about their fate.
Will they be spending the rest of their lives searching space for a dimension gate which may never
appear? You are called on to make a statement to
reassure them. Have you learned the time and space
coordinates of the black hole which will, hopefully,
take you back to your own universe? If you believe
you have, turn to **216**. If you have not yet found
them, turn to **197**.

325

You continue along the road. You are entering an area of some importance, judging by the nature of the buildings around you. You pass by a machine which appears to dispense newspapers, smash it open and take a copy. You cannot understand the language, but you take it with you to give to the language lab on your return. One particularly grand-looking building looks worth a visit, and you enter.

Inside, all is still, but a voice at the entrance desk asks you who you wish to see. The voice makes you jump, but it is merely an electronic receptionist machine. You decide to start at the top and work down, on the assumption that the most important offices will be at the top of the building.

On the fourth floor you enter a room at which a figure sits slumped over a desk in front of a computer terminal. Cautiously, you walk up to him. As you approach, it is apparent that he has long been dead. His skin is rotten and he smells unpleasant. You rock him backwards into his chair while you inspect the computer console. As you do so, his eyes flick open! The three of you spring back, on guard, with phasers drawn. He smiles a smile which, if it were not for his deceased condition, could almost be described as friendly, and you announce yourselves. He nods very slowly. His VDU flickers and is active, speaking to you in an electronic voice. Symbols appear on the screen which mean nothing to you until you realize he is trying to help you choose a subject which he can provide information on! Immediately you ask whether he can help you get home. After some moments, the voice announces that due to the differences in atomic frequency, a space warp is likely to open up on Stardate 45, through a black hole.

Thanking your host for the information, you contact the ship and arrange to be beamed up at once. Turn to **130**.

Throw two dice and compare the total with your own SKILL score. If the roll *exceeds* your SKILL score, turn to **266**. If you roll a number *less than or equal to* your SKILL, turn to **12**.

327

Select one of your officers to mine the dilibrium and send him to the airlock hatch. In the airlock are jet packs and EVA (Extra Vehicular Activity) suits which enable crew members to move in space outside the ship and also provide protection against the vacuum outside.

The going is easy on the fringes of the cluster, as the asteroids move slowly and they are well spaced apart. Closer to the centre the going is more tricky. Roll one die. If you roll a 1, turn to **204**. If you roll a 6, turn to **190**. Otherwise turn to **47**.

328

The creature appears to look at you (you are not sure whether it can actually see or not) and you fire. As the blast hits its body, it rears into the air, roaring loudly – and its huge feet come down on top of you! To your despair, a *stun* blast was enough only to cause it some pain and now its massive weight has crushed you beneath it. This is the end of your adventure . . .

329

You set the ship in orbit round the large red planet. Your scanners indicate an intelligent dominant species on the planet and you try to communicate with them. After some time you establish radio contact with a being who identifies himself as Commander Domm, head of the space navy on the planet Dar-Vil. His image flicks up on the screen. He is humanoid in shape although somewhat grotesque by Earth standards. You estimate his height at over two metres and his craggy face gives you the impression that this race is somewhat aggressive. Nevertheless, he invites you and two other crew members from the *Adventure Sheet* to beam down to meet him. If you will visit the planet Dar-Vil, turn to **132**. If you wish to press onwards, turn to **316**.

330

The Ganzigite reacts quickly, pressing a button on its belt. Your chosen staff member leaps forward – only to be flung back against a wall by an invisible force-field the alien has created around itself. Deduct 1 point from your staff member's SKILL and 2 points from his STAMINA.

The alien warns you not to try such foolish ploys and demands to be taken to the bridge while you follow his ship to the Ganzig starbase. Reluctantly, you agree. Turn to **202**.

331

You drop out of hyperspace near a small, black planet. Scanners cannot locate life on its surface. Would you like to beam down anyway to investigate (turn to **97**) or ignore this planet and proceed towards another (turn to **104**)?

332

Your Science Officer has been observing the aliens and has noticed that something is strange and not quite natural about them. He believes that these creatures may not be creatures at all – that in fact you are on a planet controlled by androids, artificially manufactured robots made to resemble living creatures. He suggests you try setting your communicator to a jamming frequency, which you do. To your surprise, all the aliens in the room are suddenly frozen, as if time is standing still! While they are all transfixed, you quickly leave the room. Turn to **160**.

333

As you approach the double star, your scanners indicate that its third planet should be capable of sustaining life. You guide the ship into orbit round this planet. Further scanning confirms positive signs of intelligent life, and you send out an all-frequency message. A short while later, a message comes back from the planet.

You switch to the screen and a strange face appears. Hairless and brown in colour, the alien wears a multi-coloured tunic and introduces herself – she appears to be a female – as Dilane, Extra-Terrestrial Communications Officer of the planet Macommon. Her voice is extremely pleasant, and has a certain musical quality. You explain that you are searching for a way back to your own universe, and you ask whether she may be able to help. She appears to contact someone for a few moments and then says, 'I think we may be able to help you. You are welcome to beam down and visit us.' Will you take her up on her offer (turn to **39**) or would you prefer to leave orbit and continue onwards (turn to **141**)?

334

At this range you cannot miss, and the creature slumps over its table. Excited jabberings at the door indicate that you have been observed and whatever was watching you has run off up the road. As you look around the room you are in, you hear noises. A crowd of aliens are approaching, apparently angry at your attack. You feel it prudent to leave this planet and return to the ship. Turn to **290**.

335

You relate your exchange with Commander M'k Tel. The alien is suspicious and orders that you accompany him to the nearest starbase. If you will follow him as he orders, turn to **15**. If you refuse, you will have to attack his ship (remember any penalties enforced by your last encounter).

Alien ship WEAPONS STRENGTH 8   SHIELDS 12

For ship-to-ship combat rules, turn to **341** but *re-*

member this reference so that you can return afterwards. If you defeat the Ganzigites, turn to **185**.

336
You reset your onward course. Will you head for the purple star ahead (turn to **44**) or for the double star (turn to **333**)?

337
Using an EVA (Extra Vehicular Activity) suit, your Medical Officer examines the body of one of the victims. She finds that the man has been poisoned. The planet below must have some sort of poisonous gas in its atmosphere and this has now been carried back to the ship. Will you:

Get the MO to search for an antidote and treat the crew?	Turn to **223**
Evacuate the air from all the affected sections?	Turn to **284**

338
The path twists on ahead and you soon arrive at another fork. Will you take the right-hand fork (turn to **20**) or the left-hand fork (turn to **166**)?

339
You will never know whether or not this was the correct black hole. Perhaps it was your angle of entry, or maybe it was your speed, or even the information you have. Whatever the error, the *Traveller* never emerges from the void. Your mission has been unsuccessful.

You regain consciousness and look around to find that other crew members are doing the same. You instruct your navigation officer to report on your position and switch the screen to visual. As the picture clears, you can see space in front of you. Is this your own universe?

In the distance, you can just make out a large familiar-looking object. Your communications officer shouts excitedly: 'Captain! I am picking up a signal coming from somewhere ahead of us. They claim to be sub-station Einstein! I think we have made it!'

Switching the message to visual, you are soon able to confirm that the message is indeed coming from one of your own sub-stations. You have made it through the black hole and back into your own universe. The crew gather round to congratulate you. You have successfully guided the *Traveller*, and its crew, safely home.

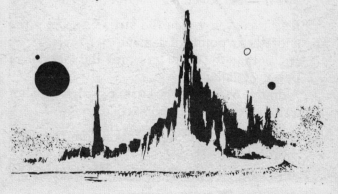

IMPORTANT! Note the number of the reference you have just come from before you read on. You will need to return to that reference.

Ship-to-ship combat is conducted as follows:

1. Ships attack each other in turn. Unless instructions are given otherwise, you will attack the alien ship first.
2. Roll two dice for your attack on the alien ship. Compare the total rolled with your ship's WEAPONS STRENGTH.
3. If the total is *equal to or higher than* your ship's WEAPONS STRENGTH, you have missed; proceed to Step 7.
4. If the total is *lower than* your ship's WEAPONS STRENGTH, you have scored a direct hit; proceed to Step 5.
5. To determine how much damage a hit has done, roll two dice again but this time compare the total with the alien ship's SHIELDS score. If the number rolled is:

Equal to or lower than the SHIELDS score – the shot does 2 points of damage
Higher than the SHIELDS score – the shot does 4 points of damage
A double 6 – ignore the SHIELDS score; the shot automatically does 6 points of damage

6. Deduct the resulting damage from the alien ship's SHIELDS score.
7. It is now the alien's turn to attack you. The

procedure is exactly the same but in reverse. Roll two dice. Compare the total rolled with the alien's WEAPONS STRENGTH. If *lower*, a hit has been scored on your ship. To determine how much damage will be deducted from your SHIELDS, roll two dice again, compare the total rolled with your ship's SHIELDS score and make deductions as instructed in Step 5 above.

8. Return to Step 2 and continue the fight. Each ship attacks in turn until one ship's SHIELDS are reduced to zero. When this happens any further damage will cause that ship to explode in space.

After a battle, your SHIELDS will have been damaged. They will only be repaired if you stop at a spaceport; but not all spaceports will allow you to repair the ship. When repairs are allowed, you will be told in the text.

Now return to the reference you have just come from and fight your battle.

IMPORTANT! Note the number of the reference you have just come from before you read on. You will need to return to that reference.

Hand-to-hand combat is conducted as follows:

1. Combat is simultaneous. Non-weapon fighting is a series of clashes in which one combatant will do damage to the other. In the following steps the term 'alien' applies to any creature which is fighting against you or a member of your crew. The term 'you' applies either to you personally if you are fighting the alien yourself or to any of your crew members, etc., that you have chosen to fight against the alien.

2. Roll two dice. Add the alien's SKILL score to the roll. The resulting total is the alien's *Attack Strength*.

3. Roll two dice again. Add your SKILL score to the roll. The resulting total is your *Attack Strength*.

4. If the alien's *Attack Strength* is higher than yours, it has inflicted damage on you.

5. If your *Attack Strength* is higher than the alien's, you have inflicted damage on it.

6. If both *Attack Strengths* are equal, both attacks have missed. Start the next attack round starting from Step 2 above.

7. Damage (injury, wounds) is represented by deductions from the injured party's STAMINA score. If you have damaged the alien, deduct 2 points from its STAMINA score. If it has damaged you, deduct 2 points from your own STAMINA score.

8. Start the next attack round (repeat Steps 2–7 above) and continue until one of the com-

batants' STAMINA score is reduced to zero (death).

9. If an option to surrender is given in the text, you may stop the battle so as to save you from further damage.

If a hand-to-hand combat situation has odd numbers (i.e. the sides are not equal) you will have to determine who attacks who. Everyone must fight an opponent, but if, for example, three of you fight four aliens, there will be one alien left over and you must dice to decide who the spare alien attacks. You do this by rolling a die for each of your party; the highest roll is attacked by the spare alien in addition to the one he is already fighting. If there are more crew members than aliens (e.g. after you have already killed an alien in the battle), you yourself may decide which of the aliens your spare crew member fights.

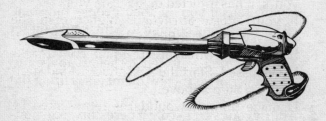

If two (or more) crew or aliens are attacking a single opponent, you must treat this as 'a normal battle with an extra attack'. Decide who the 'normal battle' will take place between (your choice) and resolve this Attack Round in the normal way. Then throw dice to determine the extra attacker's *Attack Strength* and compare this with the *Attack Strength* you have just rolled for the defender. If the extra attacker's *Attack Strength* is higher, normal damage has been inflicted. If the defender has a higher *Attack Strength*, nothing happens – the extra attacker does not take damage. Try this out; it is not as complicated as it sounds.

Now return to the reference you have just come from and fight your battle.

343

IMPORTANT! Note the number of the reference you have just come from before you read on. You will need to return to that reference.

Phaser combat is conducted as follows:
1. First of all your phaser(s) must be set either to *stun* or *kill*. You risk antagonizing some alien populations if you kill their people, but some aliens are strong enough to withstand a hit set only to stun.
   N.B. The 'you' referred to below applies to whichever of your crew members is firing the phaser.
2. Adjust your SKILL score if necessary (e.g. non-security crew deduct 3 from SKILL in battle).
3. Roll two dice. You may be instructed in the text to add to or to make deductions from this roll according to target size, whether it is moving, etc. Make any adjustments and then compare the number rolled with your SKILL score.

4. If the adjusted number is *higher than or equal to* your SKILL score, you have missed.

5. If the adjusted number is *lower than* your SKILL score, you have hit your target and either stunned or killed it.

6. If your target is an alien with a phaser or other range weapon – and you have not yet killed this alien – then repeat Steps 2–5 above to see whether the alien kills you (all aliens set phasers on *kill* unless described otherwise in the text).

7. Both sides fire in turn by repeating Steps 2–6 above until one side is either stunned or killed.

8. If more than two combatants are 'shooting it out', you may decide – before shooting – which of the aliens each of your crew members is aiming at. You must also determine who the aliens are firing at. This is most conveniently done by assigning each of your crew members a number between one and six and then tossing a die for each alien to determine who he is shooting at (if there are less than six crew members, roll again if the number has not been assigned).

If you die as a result of a phaser battle, your mission has ended. So beware getting into phaser fights; they are quick and deadly.

Now return to the reference you have just come from and fight your battle.